THE
WONDERFUL
STORY CLUB

COOL!

ShinJi's file

No one is to have a peep.

This file is full of wonderful stories by ShinJi.

Get Permission before you look. ShinJi Park.

THE WONDERFUL STORY CLUB

ShinJi Park

SANZINI

CONTENTS

The Story Club

Laura Nana woke because of by a loud noise that didn't stop. Laura looked at her clock near her bed and realised it was 10. So her parents must have gone to work by now. She opened her curtains to find out what the noise was. There was never such a big truck as big as this one! Not in Park Lane.

The big blue truck drove on a little bit further than stopped. Laura was so surprised that such a massive truck was owned by somebody living in Park Lane. Park Lane was a peaceful road and cars weren't allowed. There were parking spaces for those who owned a car and lived in Park Lane.

A Chinese man stepped out of the truck then a English woman then followed a little girl who looked tired.

Aha! Somebody was moving in to number fifteen.

The biggest house in Park Lane with a nice front garden and back garden. However Laura was not happy or sad to see a girl moving in. There were loads of children in Park Lane. Well, seven. The houses were owned by old men and ladies. There were families with no children and in next doors there was a

American who lived alone with a dog called Huggy. She visited him a lot. Next to her house on right, there lived a family with a baby girl. Laura didn't mind one bit about Catherine (the baby girl) screaming.

Laura was 13. She lived with her parents and gran in number 2 Park Lane. She had lived there all her life.

Laura never bothered with breakfasts. She decided she would give those people a hand. Maybe she would meet the girl. The morning air was lovely. Laura ran all the way to number 15.

"Hello! We've moved to number 15. Nice to meet you." the man said as if he was expecting her. But Laura was glad that her new neighbors were friendly.

"Yes, lovely to meet you too. I'm Laura Nana. I live in number two. Just over there." Laura tried to make her voice as excited as the man but she couldn't. Obviously she wasn't that excited.

"Ooooh! A visitor! I'm Shian. Nice to meet you. Your name?" The woman came out of the house. The little girl was hiding behind her mum.

"She's Laura Nana. She lives in number 2. Over there." The man said grinning and went back in to the house.

"He's Cho-Harvey." Shian also said smiling.

"I was just going to give you a hand unpacking things, you know. I thought you might want some help." Laura met the shy girl's eyes. "Hi, there."

"Oh, Laura, this is my daughter Elji. She's usually shy. Say hello, Elji." Shian said, leaving Laura and Elji alone.

"You're Elighja?" Laura guessed the girl's name. She knew it was El something, Elighja was the first name that came into her head.

"Elighja? That's a good name. Elighja. It's Elji. I suppose you could call me Elighja." Elji said.

"Are you giving me a hand?" Cho-Harvey shouted to Elji.

"You can come in to give us a hand too Laura!" He added.

"Sure." Laura replied. When they were all settled down, Laura had breakfast at Elighja's.

Elighja's mum asked. "Which school does Elji have to go, Laura?"

"How old is she?"

"She's 10."

"Then she will go to Plants elementary school. A small school but very nice." Laura replied.

Now Laura was a middle school student.

"Do you go to the that school?" Elighja's father asked.

"I used to go there. But I go to Sharden middle school now."

There was a silence. Elighja's dad broke it.

"Laura, do you think you could look after Elji? We have to go to Elji's school."

"Sure."

So Elighja and Laura were left alone. Laura spotted a thick paper. She picked it up. And read it out.

"Bye bye Elji. It has been a pleasure to meet you in the 'living for reading' club. We give you this award with pleasure.

From 'L. F. R' club."

"Oh, that's a club. You read a book in a week and go to the club and tell people the story." Elighja explained.

Laura thought and thought again.

'Yes, I'll make a 'Story Club' during the holiday!'

Laura told her idea to Elighja and she suggested right away. So they decided to go around the houses to ask to join the club.

First they went to Jack Reel's house number 17. Jack himself came out.

"Hi, Laura! Good morning!" Jack welcomed Laura.

"Good morning Jack. This is Elighja at number 15. And wanna joining our Story Club?" Laura asked.

"Sure, Great idea!" Jack replied.

That morning Laura and Elighja went to Ellen Frank, Trevor, Alex Hall and Kaylee Dale's houses. They all decided to join the 'Story Club' and promised to meet up tomorrow.

The Jewels in the Garden

It was snowing day. Chris Parker was very bored. He rang his friend Ben. Ben's mother Mrs. Edward replied.

"Oh hello, Chris. Do you want Ben?"

Chris was shy to all the adult his face went red.

He said,"Er... Mrs. Edward, er, can Ben come to my house?"

Mrs. Edward replied.

"Oh, Chris, don't be so shy and call me Zoe. And of course Ben can play with you. Is Mrs. Parker there?" Chris was so excited to answer Mrs. Edward. So he gave the phone to his mother.

"Mum, Mrs. Edwards."

He ran off to his bedroom. Soon Ben came. His mother was there too. Mrs. Edward said to Mrs. Parker.

"Ben was too bored, he couldn't go anywhere without me even he was year 5 because it's snowing day and just in time Chris phoned us." She smiled. Mrs. Parker smiled too. Chris came down. He said bravely this time.

"Hello, Zoe. Mum, can I go out to garden with Ben?"

"Of course." Mrs. Parker replied, a putting some biscuit in a bowl.

"Have a cup of tea and you shall go out boys." Both they had hot chocolate and went out to the garden.

"Ben, I got a secret in the garden. I and you share it."

Chris began to dig the edge of the garden.

Ben said wearing a coat,

"What are you doing Chris? Are you collecting some snow to build a snowman or a snow ball?"

Chris just smiled and he said, "You wait and see."

Whilst Chris dug the edge of the garden, Ben made a big, big snow ball. Later Chris said, "Ben, follow me."

Before Ben could say a word, Chris said,"You will have to keep this secret well, Ben."

Ben followed. He looked so puzzled. He carried the snow-ball with him. Chris went into the ground where he dug. They jumped in and walked straight.

Later Chris said suddenly, "Oh no, I forgot to bring water with me."

Ben said looking at the snowball,

"I got some water I can melt this snowball, but why do you

need water?"

"For these," replied Chris.

In a shock Ben saw jewels. Ben gave snowball to Chris, Chris melted it on a necklace.

He cried, "It's Harrieta's jewels. We have to give it back to her. Poor Harrieta."

Then Ben smiled he said,

"You are such a good boy."

So two boys went out with jewels in their pocket. They went to Harrieta's house. Ben knocked the door. Harrieta opened the door. She welcomed boys. "Hi, Chris and Ben."

Chris and Ben gave the jewels to Harrieta.

Ben said,"Hi, Harrieta, we found these in Chris's garden. Chris found it."

Harrieta shouted in delight.

"Thank you very much. You are kindest boys in the world, if it wasn't Chris, I couldn't have it back. You're not like greedy Jake. Oh, Thank you so much. Do you want have tea with us?"

Chris was too shy to speak so Ben said,

"No, thank you, we just had a tea. Bye, Harrieta."

Harrieta waved. Ben and Chris couldn't have jewels but they thought it was happiest day.

Next morning Harrieta came over while Ben and Chris were Playing playstation 2 in Chris's house.

"Hi, Harri!" Ben said delighted. "Wanna play as well?"

"No, I just thought of something the jewels." Harrieta said desperately.

"What about it?" Ben said carelessly.

"You've got it back, Harri. One missing?" Chris added.

"No, you two, you've got to listen! Well in fact I have got a few missing! That's not all bothering me." Harrieta was loosing her temper.

"You two! Switch that Playstation off. You've got to take some notice!"

Chris got up.

"Okay, I give up. I'll switch it off. There, What's troubling you?" Chris said when he had turned off the game and was ready to listen to Harrieta. Ben did the same action.

"Didn't you steal it Chris, My jewels were in the living room... no! Actually, it was in my bag, wasn't it? Anyway Chris did you steal it?" Harrieta squealed worriedly glancing towards Chris in a corner of her eye.

"Oh, Harri! Goodness gracious, you won't imagine Chris stealing it! Chris!" Ben snorted. "He never touchs somebody's property without permission." Ben said very certainly that it was not Chris's behavior.

Chris didn't seem so sure. But he knew he didn't do it. He only nodded, half frozen.

"I'm not accusing you. Of course not!" Harrieta said looking at the worried face.

"Who could have done it then?" Chris was now back to normal.

"Well, it must be action of somebody that doesn't like Chris." Harrieta said thoughtfully and calmly.

"Why's that?" Ben asked with an odd face.

"Then who else would steal the jewels and hide it in Chris's backgarden?" The person obviously and probably didn't want the jewels. But he wanted Chris to get into trouble. And I think somebody must have been jealous of Chris being friends with me. The preson really wanted me to dislike you or maybe hate you. Fortunately I know you too well!"

Harrieta finished her long long story. Harrieta smiled proud of herself.

"You are clever, Harrieta." Ben muttered.

"But who hates me?" Chris said, he didn't think about Harrieta the way Ben did. He was actually impressed by Hattieta's theory.

"That's what I was thinking Chris." Harrieta ignored Ben yawning fakely one after another.

"You hardly get involved in anything that annoys somebody or make them hate you." Harrieta spoke. "He's a teacher's pet all right!" somebody sneered.

It was Jake Mason. Jake Mason is Harri's brother. Ben had some enmity between Jake and him.

"What are you doing here, Mason? You weren't invited. Go away. This is my house!"

Jake went out shutting the door with a bang.

"You don't think, it's Jake, do you? After all he is a brother of mine. He is stupid, greedy and idiotic about everything. But I don't think he stole the jewels." She said nervously.

"Dunno." Chris replied very shocked indeed. Even Ben was confused.

Harrieta spoke, "I'm sure it's not Jake's behavior. Think of it. Jake and I are one family. And even though if Jake did steal it, it won't matter very much. I don't think..."

"Yes, but we'll keep on eye open. It is only 30% that it is Jake." Chris answered.

"Yeah." Ben agreed.

Today was school day. Chris and Ben walked to school together. Ben was in a very deep thought and Chris didn't want to disturb it so they kept quiet.

At last Ben spoke."I am sure 99 percent, it's not Jake. Jake won't want a necklace neither earrings. It will be a girl's behavior who doesn't really like you and..."

"It could be somebody living close to me." Chris interrupted.

"Somebody living near us... Silvia, Helen, Christoper, Katie and Beeky. That's all." Ben said.

Harrieta wonders who stole the jewels and the three become detectives. They think it over and over again in Ben and Chris's den.

Harrieta thinks it's somebody who doesn't like her much and doesn't like Chris much either.

At school they spot Kathryn(Kathy) wearing one of Harri's jewels. (Kathy is very normal girl.)

That afternoon Harri, Chris and Ben invite her to the den because they know it is Kathy. But Kathy says that Bethany(Beth) gave it to her.

So next day, they (Chris, Ben, Harri and Kathy) met at school. (Kathy becomes a member of the detectives.)

Beth comes at school and explains all about it to her friends. :Beth couldn't help it. Beth is poor and everybody sneered because Beth was poor. So she wanted to show jewels to her friends. She apologizes at Harri seriously and Harri forgives her. Beth becomes a member of the detectives. After they experience some troubles, they become the best of friends at the school.

What a Surprise!

One fine afternoon, Rachel was reading a letter in the garden. It was very fine October afternoon. Rachel had a letter. It was very strange letter. The postman didn't give this letter through postbox. A beautiful white bird gave this letter through window. So, No one knew Rachel had a letter. She read it again, because it was too hard to understand.

It says:

Dear, Rachel
Hello, Dear Rachel
You are invited to my land. Everyone will welcome you heartfully. I will tell you how to come. On 5th December evening, make a snowman for Molly not to see you. After you finish making snowman, pour your tea to snowman and hold it at other hand. That's it. See you later.

When she finished reading it, Molly came out. Quickly Rachel put her letter in her pocket. Molly was a very lazy and she was Rachel's sister.

Molly said, "Come in for tea, my little servant." Rachel said angrily, "Don't call me your little servant, I'm not your little servant. You might be my servant, but I'm not and no one calls servant for tea, Molly. I shall not go for tea, thank you."

Molly said, "Mum wants you. You must go in, or you will get in to a trouble, Rachel." And Molly went in. But Rachel's mother came out this time.

She said, "What's the matter, Rachel, I think you're worrying something or what's up dear?"

Rachel replied, "I'm angry with Molly, mum, she calls me little servant."

Her mum stared at Molly angrily and turned to Rachel. "Don't you want tea? I made chocolate cake. I will have a word with Molly. Rachel, do you want tea?"

"No, thank you."

And her mum went in.

At last, 5th December came.

The snow was falling. She still remembered the letter. She didn't want to go alone. So, she called Emily.

Emily replied.

"Hello?"

Rachel said, quite worring if Emily says 'No'.

Rachel said,"Do you want to go on a journey with me this evening?"

"I'd love to, Rachel. I will go with my bike at evening. See you."

Evening came very quickly. Rachel started making snow-man. When she finished, Molly gave her hot chocolate and a piece of cake. Emily came in.

Rachel said,"Hold my hands tightly, Emily. We are starting an Adventure."

She poured her tea to snowman and the other hand held Emily's hand.

What a surprise !

They flew off. About thirty minutes later, They saw a lot of kind and peaceful crowds.

Emily cried in amazement, "Rachel, Isn't it great, How did you know it? Did these people invite you?" Rachel said, "Amazing, yes, they invited me. There's Santa. It's Santaland, where Santa makes their toys. It's really really Wonderful."

Everyone cheered them as they went by and they came to a room. It was marvellous. The room was full of toys, sweets, cakes and everything they wanted. They ate pizzas, spaghettis, sweets and cakes.

They were too tired. So, they went to sleep.

Next morning they went to the swimming pool in their room and played golf.

They ate, played, cheerfully and slept peacefully.

Next morning they woke up. But what a surprise!, They were in their own bedroom.

Emily and Rachel told the adventure to their family. But no one ever believed an exciting and fantastic journey which happened on a special day.

The Saturday Fair

Emily was sitting on an armchair one morning. It was a very sunny morning. Emily was watching her Siamese cat, Bobby playing with a small ball. Emily had bought the cat someday.

"I'm bored!" Emily complained to her mother as she came into the room.

"Well, maybe Emily, you could help me by drying those clothes outside." Emily's mum said holding out a basket full of clothes.

"No way! That's even more boring than sitting here, watching, Bobby," Emily winged.

"Emily, if you don't want to help, then I don't know." and she went away. Emily kept watching Bobby what she called 'catwatching'. She drifted off in to daydreams often. Emily was a sort of girl who could not keep still very long and could not ever concentrate on one thing.

"Mum~." She called again.

"Yes?"

"What day is it, today?" Emily had just thought of something she could do.

"Saturday, love." Her mother replied, coming in with some coffee.

"Mum, I just thought of something really really good. Couldn't we go to the Saturday Fair, please!" Emily begged.

"That's quite a good idea actually. I need a break myself. It is such a nice day to miss all the fun out." Mum said smiling.

"But Emily you wash and change your clothes and do your hair again."

"Thanks mum!" Emily shouted and she ran to get ready.

In a second, Mum and Emily were walking to the Saturday Fair.

When they arrived there, they met Rosie and Wendy and their mums.

All six of them agreed to split up into threes and meet at the gates at 2 o'clock.

The three girls, Rosie, Wendy and Emily and three mums together. The three girls looked for their favourite stall which was sweet stall, clothes stall, name tag stall and bouncy castle.

Well, it wasn't exactly the girls' favourites but Rosie and Wendy's. Rosie and Wendy always came to the fair every Saturday. Wendy came every Saturday to have fun but also because her dad was the Saturday Fair manager. Rosie came to the town fair every Saturday and Thursday because she was a bit posh and everything.

There were town fairs every Monday, Wednesday, Thursday and Saturday. On Monday, Wednesday and Thursday's fairs there weren't as many stalls as there were on Saturdays. But still it was a great fun.

Emily and Wendy wanted to go to the sweet stall. But Rosie wanted to go to the name tag stall.

"Well, Rosie, buy your name tag and come back to our sweet stall. We will be waiting for you here." said Emily and they parted.

Minutes and minutes passed but Rosie still didn't come.

"Where is Rose? She can't take this long to find her name. Surely she knows her name?"

Emily began to complain.

"Hang on! Hang on, Em, Rosie doesn't know where this sweet stall is. And we don't know where the name tag stall is!" Wendy pointed out.

"Oh no! You wait here, Wendy. Just in case. I'll look for Rosie."

Emily set off.

The Saturday fair was huge. It was the town business square where the town fairs were held. Emily decided to ask someone because she had no idea where the name tag stall was.

"Excuse me, Do you know where the name tag stall is?"

"Sorry, honey, I don't have a clue."

So Emily tried someone else.

"Excuse me, Do you know where the name tag stall is?"

"Er... It's quite far. Go straight on. When you see the bouncy castle, turn left. Go straight. Turn left again when you see the fruit stall."

"Thank you."

Emily walked on.

At the name tag stall, Rosie was struggling to find the sweet stall also. But she didn't wait at the name tag stall cleverly. She walked on to find the stall.

Back at the sweet stall Wendy's legs were aching, and she was getting bored. She decided to just pop in to the nearest clothes stall to try some clothes. She tried three outfits and bought an outfit.

The search went on. Well, sort of Rosie had managed to find Wendy at the clothes stall. But Emily had not arrived yet. Rosie and Wendy decided it would be the best if they stayed here and waited for Emily.

"Suppose Emily found the name tag stall and she cannot find you there. You know Emily and how determined she is on everything. She will keep on searching until she finds you." Wendy pointed out again as usual.

"Good point." Rosie agreed. "I know the way to the name tag stall and to here, so you stay here. I'll be searching for Emily." and the search went on again.

The time passed by very quickly. It was 1:45.

The girls' mums were waiting by the gates. Wendy realized it was nearly 2 o'clock. She saw her mum very quickly. A tall woman with red hair. Wendy decided to go and tell them.

Wendy ran as fast as she could go looking straight at the red hair trying not to lose track of them. When she had arrived to the mums, Wendy was so exhausted she could hardly speak. But she managed to speak before the adults could ignore her.

"Mum ! Do... listen. This is so awfully important. Well, as you see there is no one next to me. Doesn't happen to be Rose and Em. They're lost." Wendy finished off.

"How did that happen? Oh my word! Rose! Rosy-Posy! Wendy do tell me! Wendy, please!" Rosie's mum began to panic.

Wendy couldn't help giggling. It was a pretty funny sight. Rosie's mum's blonde hair swinging as Rosie's mum jumped up and down.

"Well," Wendy began, opening her mouth as wide to stop her self giggling.

"To put it easily, it's like this. Rose wanted to go to name tag stall, me and Em wanted to go to sweet stall so, we separated and told Rose to come back to us. She didn't, so Em went to look for Rose. But Rose came back to the sweet stall. We waited for Em. But wherever Em was she didn't come, so Rose is out there somewhere looking for Em. And here I am."

Wendy said still having to stop a sec to open her mouth wide.

"The girls are not old enough to be responsible for themselves." Emily's mum muttered under her breath.

"Let's not waste anymore time and go to the loud speaker looking for Em and Rose." Wendy's mum said cheerfully, because her own daughter was back and next to her. So they ran up to the loud speaker and Wendy spoke.

Ladies and gentlemans,
ATTENTION!
SEEN EITHER 9 year old girls
Rose Matz or Em Daisy!
If you do tell them to come to the Gates Now!

Rosie came immediately but Emily didn't.

Mrs. Daisy was so worried that she could have rang the police and the ambulance. However Mrs. Mattheus (Matz) was so happy.

Wendy's mum hissed, "Can't you look a little sad?" Mrs. Matz did try to look sad but she still had the beam on her face.

But fortunately a young teenager did find Emily sitting on a bench and she took her to the gates. Emily felt so tired and hungry. When she got to the gates and saw her own mother she only had the strength to say "hi", Mrs. Daisy thanked the young woman holding Emily's hands tightly.

Emily, Rosie and Wendy and their mums went to a Chinese restaurant and had lunch.

Then they went back to their own house.

"Had a nice day, Emily?" mum asked cheerily.

Emily nodded uncertainly.

"We could go there another Saturday if you want," Mrs. Daisy said.

She did have a lot of work to do on Saturdays. But she knew how much her daughter wanted to go to fairs and cinemas, shopping centres and that sort of thing on weekends.

"That would be great, mum. But I don't think Saturday fairs!" Emily said smiling. Then she winked to Bobby.

The Silly Rachel

One day Rachel was sitting in her room. She just woke up. She said, looking at her watch, "Today is Thursday. Let me think. I have no lessons today. I have no meetings and I don't want to stay in the house. Mum and Dad are going to work. I know, I can play with Amy. I will call her right now."

But as she went down stairs she said, "Amy is going to ride horse today at 9 o'clock. What time is it? 8:30? She will prepare her horse riding thing and ready to go. Oh dear."

She went to her room. She thought deeply then said, "It's 9 o'clock. It's a bit early but if I go with my bike, it will be about 10 o'clock. Good. I will play golf."

Then she prepared all things she needed, "Do I need some balls? Yes, I will take mine. I have to play for balls too. I don't want to spend this money on a ball really. I will take mine." She went with her bike.

At last about half an hour later, she arrived.

She started playing golf with her yellow balls. Suddenly she heard someone saying, "Hi, Rachel, Oh, Where did you get yellow balls from? Did you get it from the machine? Lovely." It was Emily.

She replied, "Those are mine, Emily. I got it from MARY'S Golf Shop."

Emily said, "You silly girl, Rachel. How can you get it back later when you finished?"

Rachel said picking another yellow ball, "Don't worry Em. I can go to the field and get it. It's easy to find it, Emily."

Emily said laughing, "Are you joking? Rachel, You can't go to that field, because a ball might hit you. It's dangerous, Rachel. You have to wait until the machine comes and collects the balls. And stand inside machine and see if somebody get yellow ball, then you can have it. How many balls did you have? Rachel?"

Rachel replied, "That's silly idea Em. I can't spend all afternoon here and anyway I've got four balls left, sorry I meant I had ten balls."

Emily said, a little being worried, "Never mind, Rachel, I don't care if you hurt."

Rachel started playing golf. This one went far and far. At

last she had finished and went to the field. Easily she found six balls. When she went far, she was hit by a ball and was very hurt. So she went back there. She said to Mr. Kampery. He was the owner of golf range.

Rachel said, "Excuse me, Mr. Kampery, Can you help me?"

He replied, "Of couse, girl."

Rachel said, "I played golf with my balls when I finished went to the field to have my yellow balls. When I found six I was hit by a ball. I can't find any and my back hurts. Please help me."

Mr. Kampery said, "I will look at the machine later when the collecting machine finishes."

Rachel said, "When does the collecting machine go round to collect the balls?"

"After 4 hours."

"4 hours? Oh, no. Please do it quickly. It's not mine. It's my ugly lazy sister Molly's. Please."

"No, it's your fault. Excuse, Rachel, come tomorrow."

Rachel said sighing, "All right. I will come tomorrow."

At home, She had to stand outside because she touched other person's thing.

Next morning she got it back and never used their own balls

and never touched other person's thing.

How Silly Rachel Was!

The Wooden Primary School 6H

Mr. Jones's Lost Watch

Chapter 1

Kate was sitting in her seat, doing nothing. She whispered to her friend Michael.

"It's boring, nothing interesting happens in Mrs. Pacon's class. bo~~~ ring."

Then Herron said, "Why don't you get on with your work."

Michael whispered angrily. "Shut up ! You are..."

"EXCUSE ME 6H. What are you staring at, Michael, and Herron , did you find funny about it?"

"Em ... Actually no!"

"Be silent, get on with your work."

Then Michael carried on. "You naughty nau~~ghty girl."

The bell rang.

Kate and Michael shouted. "Yes ~ Yes ~Ye~s" and they went to the playground. Michael and Kate were talking about how boring it was.

Then a girl called Mary said, "Why don't you play happily in the playground?"

Kate answered, "I'm not meaning that just a lessons boring. In the school whole things are boring, nothing interesting happens in Wooden Primary School."

Michael nodded and said, "One more reason why school isn't funny is that there's a silly girl calling Herron."

Chapter 2

Next morning they went to the school. It was noisy than yesterday, but most of them were talking about a poster.

Michael saw a lot of people were gathering around a quiet area and they went to see what happened.

There was a big poster. There was a photo of their Head Teacher Mr. Jones.

And it was said :

> IF ANYONE FOUND MY LOST WATCH, I PROMISE I WILL GIVE YOU A BRIL-LIANT PRIZE.

After a lesson they tried to find a watch. Now the lesson

wasn't boring at all.

They even went to the toilet. Kate, Women's toilet, Michael, Men's toilet, it wasn't there. They went to the computer room.

Then both yelled "WE HAVE FOUND THE WATCH."

They went to the Mr. Jones's room.

Chapter 3

When they went to the Mr. Jones's room, there were already two girls talking about their favourite.

It was Herron and Pete. Pete was her best friend. Then Mr. Jones noticed Kate and Michael.

"Hello?" You two, What do you want, Mike and Katy?"
said Mr. Jones.

Michael replied, "We don't want anything, sir. We want to give you something which is your favourite watch, Here Mr. Jones."

Mr. Jones was surprised.

Very Surprised.

Chapter 4

He looked at Herron and Pete and looked at Kate and Michael.

"Where did you find it from Herron, Pety?"

Herron replied, she looked confident.

"We found it at the library between two books, didn't we pete"

"Er...ye...yes."

Mr. Jones asked to Michael and Kate.

"Then you two where did you find it from?"

Both replied, "We found it from computer room."

Chapter 5

Then he asked to Herron and Pete.

"Which book was between the watch Herron, Pete? Point to it."

Herron pointed book about Earth and Pete pointed about Country.

And Mr. Jones said, "You liar you both pointing different book! Then where is this watch from ? Pety?"

Pete replied quietly, "That watch's from...

Herron's father."

Chapter 6

They both looked so sorry and they had no play time for a week. Michael and Kate had a choice and both decided their present will be a party. Mary had a cake there saying 'boring lesson!'

It was amazing party and after this matter in the school nothing was boring. They loved to come to the school.

The Trip!

It was Wednesday and 6H was on a trip. Mrs. Pacon was choosing a partner. She was choosing boy and girl. She started "Herron, Jack, Pete, Ashley, Kate, Michael, Mary, Callum......" and so on.

"Herron's with Jack, Herron's with Jack.." Michael sang and Kate giggled because Jack was a fat boy, and he was always sick when he got on the coach they went.

Michael and Kate sat back of the coach, at the back of the coach there were 6 seat Michael sat at right Kate next Herron, Jack, Pete and Ashley.

Mary was Kate's friend as well. She sometimes joined Michael and Kate.

Now the coach was half way and Herron was sleeping when Jack went "OOPS" he vomited at Pete and Herron. Because he was looking at Pete, then he vomited. So, he didn't try to vomitted on Pete but when he turned, he vomited at Herron. Ashley went to call Mrs. Pacon.

Mrs. Pacon was already sleeping!

Ashley shouted. Pete and Herron didn't know what to do, so didn't Jack either. So they were staring at each other.

Then a girl Amy who is enemy of Herron and Pete, she shouted "Ashley, Oey! Ashley, it's none of your business is it?"

Ashley said quietly, "Er...er..."

Then Michael and Kate sang "Ashley loved Herron, Ashley loved Pety, Ashley loves Herron and Pety."

When they sang a song, Mrs. Pacon woke up.

"What's happening here?" then she called Mary.

Mary went front looked sad. She looked like she couldn't say. She didn't do anything. So, Kate hands went straight up.

"Yes Kate," said Mrs. Pacon.

"Mrs. Pacon, I'm sure that Mary doesn't do anything. She was just sitting," said Kate.

"Then did you do it, Kate?" asked Mrs. Pacon.

"No, I never did, Mrs.," replied Kate.

"Yes, you did, you two Michael, Katy," shouted Herron.

"What did we do, you STUPID?" yelled Michael.

She replied, "Can't you remember, why aren't you thinking? Mike, you sang."

Then Kate argued. "You, listen. Is... Something wrong with singing, eh? Am I right? Have you got it?"

Then Herron looked so angry "Stop lying please. Can you say the truth right now? It isn't a normal thing. You are singing about Ashley. You are annoying him, don't you?"

"Stop It, Herron," yelled Mrs. Pacon. "What happened Mary? You will know because Katy said you didn't do it."

Then Mary began.

"It happened when Jack vomited. Something vomited went to Herron and Pety. When Ashley tried to get a tissue, then Amy said, 'It's none of your business'." Then she stopped and looked sad. She sighed deeply and carried on. "Then Mike and Kate sang about Ashley that Ashley loves two girl."

Then Herron shouted, "True, Mary's best, nothing wrong with me and Pete."

"Be Quiet Children. We arrived at playground, let's get out. you must go with your partner. Must," said Mrs. Pacon.

"Yes, Pete."

"I can't. Can you see something wrong with me?" yelled Pete.

Mrs. Pacon answered, "Then... em..no idea, just go with Jack and her." "Yes."

Herron cried with excitement.

"So, Ashley have to go with Mary and Callum."

They went out of the bus saying thank you to the driver and

they went.

Herron, Pete, Jack was front of the line and Michael and Kate was in the end of the line. In front of them was Mary, Ashley and Callum. When they went in from gate there was a large Maze, it was brilliant.

Some people lost their way but others were having prizes.

Callum said, "Can we go to Maze please please Mrs. Pacon."

Mrs. Pacon said firmly, "No, we can't spend all time on the Maze children." and they were forward. Mary was talking to boys to stop annoying her.

Michael and Kate whispered, they crawled to the Maze and they were at the the Maze now!

The man said, "Hiya, Money. £1. please.

Michael had 80p and Kate had £3. So, Michael borrow Kate's £1 and they went in to the Maze.

After five minutes they were lost the way, Michael saw someone winning prize.

Class was in shop. Mary was calling "Katy!, Mike!" but they wasn't there and she told it to the teacher and they all search for Michael and Kate except Herron and Pete.

And that person was Mr. Lee and he was doing it again. Kate had an idea. She whispered. The man came near them and they followed. They stayed at the end of the Maze. They hide somewhere and after 1 minutes, they won prize. So they went to search for Class.

Class were sitting having rest, then Amy shouted, "Mike's Here, So do Kate."

And they had no play time for a week, but it was such a Brilliant Day!! (for Mike and Kate)

The three all did work hard and went back to school and told Mrs. Bumble and some children, what had happened. Mrs. Bumble ringed Michael and Katy. They had no play time for a week. But had enough sleep so they wasn't so sad!

But the one thing they were worried about was they had three enemies. It was Ashley, Callum and Jack.

Ashley was the captain. He made some boys to help him.

Michael said, "We have 5 enemies. Ashley, Callum, Jack, Pete and Herron. We have to make 5 people for our team."

Kate suddenly said, "Amy's coming back tomorrow. We shall ask Amy. She certainly will like it. And her best friend Georgina. I know Mary. She's our friend. What a good idea."

Michael, who was listening said, "I don't think so. We will have a lot of trips. Mary's partner will be Callum. They will hate each other and Mrs. Bumble will wonder what happened. So, she will find out about it." He continued "Look at Georgina, Katy. She is playing with Peter. I mean Pete. She will tell to Pete, what happening to us. She might tell our secret. Not, Georgina. She's not very clever. I don't think Mary and Georgina will be good member of our team. Katy, What do you think about it?"

She replied. "You are right. We will wait until tomorrow.

You, me and Amy will sort it out. Amy, she likes studying, so, she will a bit more clever, yes?" Katy said happily.

Next morning, Amy came to school then said, "Good morning. You look quite worrying Michael, what's the matter? Tell me, please. Is it about Pepsy? I'm quite angry about it. What's the matter?"

Katy suddenly asked, "What's Pepsy, Amy?"

Amy answered. "It's our enemies name, Pepsy."

Michael said, "That's what I am worrying about. Amy, Can I say something to you?"

Amy said, "Anything, Anything, Mike."

Michael came to a garden and sat down at the top of the stairs, he said "They have five people. You see. They are too many for me and Katy. So, I was trying to make some people. I thought 5 people will right because it's fair. We have thought about Mary. She's kind. But however her patner is Callum, our enemy. They will hate each other and soon Mrs. Bumble will find out. Georgina is another person we thought of. But wasn't right, because we saw her playing with Pepsy.

But still we have three. It's unfair."

The bell rang. They went in for lesson. Katy and Michael never litstened to what Mrs. Bumble was saying. Not a word.

But Amy loved lesson. She was listening carefully each word. The bell rang.

They went out for a play with Amy. They went where they sat. In a shock they saw a boy crying. He was Daniel. He was in 6H, same class as them.

Amy asked, "Why are you crying? Are you feeling not well?"

He was very brave boy. And in year four he was Michael's best friend.

Daniel replied, "Pepsy. They are annoying me. Always, yesterday morning they started annoying me, they don't leave me alone. They will searching everywhen by now."

Amy said, "Have you got friends Daniel?"

He said "No" and stoped crying.

Amy continued. "Do you want play with us? We will be nice friends for you."

He nodded and said "Thank you". He was fourth member!

They told him what was going to happen.

Then he seemed very happy and said, "I will help you." He asked, "Have you got any team name?"

Amy said "No" and decided to call "Shark" Daniel said.

Next day, "I think you said to me you need 5 people. You need one more person. How about this boy?" Katy shouted in delight.

"It's Sam, Michael. Michael, it's Sam, remember? When we were in Yr 1, he rescued you. Great. Let him be a Shark, Michael, Amy."

They soon agreed and Shark was always brave, but nothing happened except one trip.

Next day Mrs. Pacon came back and Daniel said, "Why didn't you come on Monday Mrs. Pacon?"

"I was on my holiday dear. Did you like Mrs. Bumble? Children?"

All of children said "No, No!"

Sam said, "I hate her."

Harry said, "She is too young. She said to me she is in university."

Katy said, "Very horrible. Horrible young teacher I never met a teacher like that."

Michael said, "Terrible."

Then Mrs. Pacon said, "Oh right. Good news for you all. We are having trip tomorrow. We are walking up to mountain children. I suggest you have a group of 5 people."

Pepsy cheered.

Shark cheered too.

Mary was with Georgina and Paiana and three boys. Mary looked quite sad but Katy and Michael didn't care.

Team Pepsy - Herron

Pete

Ashley

Callum

Jack

Team Shark - Mickael

Kate

Amy

Daniel

Sam

A Dangerous Trip

It was Friday. 6H was excited, because they were going to trip called Wooden Royal mountain.

Mrs. Pacon warned 6H.

"Calm down children. I must say this to you. The mountain is very dangerous. You never push somebody. Right? If you pushed somebody you will have no play time for a month or forever. Do you understand? I hope you have group of five people. Mary, have you got a group? Who is with you Mary? You seems quite unhappy."

Mary answered. "No, I'm happy. My Group is em ... Georgina, me, Paiana, Prisha, Olivio, Kevin."

Mrs. Pacon suddenly asked, "Kevin Jung? or Kevin Rider?"

Mary said smiling, "Kevin Rider. Mrs. Pacon."

Mrs. Pacon smiled too, "You have nice people in your group, Mary. Be happy dear."

Mary suddenly said, "Mrs. Pacon, Kevin have to be in the other group."

"Why?" Mrs. Pacon asked.

Mary answered, "Because you've said to us we need only 5 people but we have six."

Mrs. Pacon smiled again and said, "No problem. Right, Children. You have to come back from toilet by now and ready for our trip."

So, they lined up with groups. Pepsy was at the end of the line. In front of them was Shark. They went up to the mountain.

When they were going up, Herron and Ashley whispered something. Ashley pretended to trip over and caught Michael's foot.

Michael tripped over, he yelled. "Ouch Ouch My leg My leg, Mrs. Pacon." Michael yelled so loudly every can hear. "Herron and Ashley whispered together. I'm sure it's them. They have no play time, please."

Mrs. Pacon said looking at Michael, "Are you all right? Mrs. Bumble, did you saw what had happened? If you do please tell me. So, I can sort it out."

Mrs. Bumble replied who was following, "I saw exactly what had happened and I heard exactly what they said." She began. "That fat boy and that girl had a plan before they came up the mountain. So, the boy said, 'Shall I start?' girl, said 'Yes'." She continued. "Boy pretend he hits tripped over and caught Mike, was it? Yes. Mike's foot."

Mrs. Pacon looked a bit worried.

"Excuse me, Mrs. Bumble, Who is the boy and girl?"

Mrs. Bumble said, "Sorry, Mrs. Pacon. I didn't finished yet, I will tell you later. Then the boy pretended he hurted his leg. And now time to call their name. Ashley Brinia, Herron Malfoy, Pete Lanini."

They had no play time for 1 year and Michael hurted so badly, Michael couldn't come school by a week.

The next day Kate yelled. "Stupid things, Stupid em. Herron Malfoy, Ashley Brinia, Pete Lanini, Jack Karini, Callum Bigth."

She played with Amy and Harry. She said, "I'm quite worrying about Michael you know, he suppose to come school tomorrow. Yesterday I went to see Michael but his sister Fonny was alone in the house and she said to me. "The Doctor said he need some rest for a long time."

Amy said, "Don't worry, he will be all right. And please calm down. Katy."

Katy calmed down."Harry and Amy, Shall we go and see Miss Jean. She know what's going on with Mike. Harry do you agree?"

"Sure Kate. But the problem is that Miss Jean loves Ashley. She told me and she certainly will tell it to Mrs. Pacon."

Suddenly Daniel came. "Can I play?"

Katy said, "Of course Dan. But we are not playing. We are visiting Miss Jean to hear about Michael. Dan, Where is Sam, I want to talk to him."

Then Daniel said walking with the others, "He is in Miss Jean's office, he got a stomachache. But I don't want to visit Miss Jean, Katy. Because there is ..."

Katy said angrily, "I want information about Michael, Dan. Stay here if you don't want to come with us."

Daniel said, "I didn't finish there is Ashley and Herron. The rest is in Mr. Birk's office."

But everyone went to Miss Jean's office. So, Daniel just followed.

Harry whispered to Daniel. "Did you forgot you are in Shark's Daniel? I told Katy. Katy knows it. Don't worry, boy."

They arrived in Miss Jean's office. At the coner of the office was Ashley but there wasn't Herron there.

Katy smiled brightly and said, "Good afternoon, Miss Jean, I came to you to know something and talk with somebody in your office."

Miss Jean said quickly, "What is your question?"

Harry said because Katy was talking with Sam. "Good afternoon, Miss. Katy is wondering about Michael. She wants to know what's happening to Michael."

Miss Jean said at last tiding her desk, "Michael, still bad, his legs are recovered neatly but he need some rest. He will come back to the school later, he will not come to the school before his legs will become normal."

Daniel asked, "Where is he, then?"

Miss Jean said, "Speak politely, Young man! Michael is in his house. You are not allowed to go to Mike's house today. Fonny got headache and just went home. Ashley get on with your work. You are going to work in your classroom with Mrs. Bumble. Lesson is after about 5 minute later. Harry and others, see you then."

They all went to the playground. Katy felt Shark was lost then she shouted, "Now Sharks is lost. Michael is hurting his leg, Sam got a headache, dearness me."

Amy shouted angrily to Katy, "Katy, calm down, nothing will help us with your shouting. Sam got stomachache not headache, Kate."

Katy said nothing. She just set on a step. Others followed.

Harry who was the most clever boy sat next Katy and said, "Nothing to worry, Katy. In a minute Sam will be all right and Michael soon will be normal as he was. You still got Dan and Amy, Katy. Michael will be glad seeing your brave behavior than thinking Sharks are lost."

Katy smiled and said, "Thanks Harry. Tell me the truth, will you?"

"Of course, I will."

Katy said, "Can you be the seventh member (a secret agent like '007 movie') of Shark?"

Harry cried with delight, "Thanks Katy. That's exactly what I wanted to hear. Of course I will !"

Everyone laughed because they never had seen Harry so much excited.

The bell for hometime rang .

Amy said to Katy,"Sorry." "Sorry? Why are you sorry to me?"

"Because I shouted at you,"

Katy said shyly. "It's OK. But I was a bit naughty really."

Daniel and Harry came.

Amy said, "Can you all come to the my house? Even though Simone's coming early, my parents are in their work."

Daniel said looking at Amy, "No problem. How about coming to the my house, I have no brother or sister and Mum and Dad is in their work!"

"Very good." Everyone agreed.

So, they went to the Daniel's house. They all sat on the sofas, girls sat on a one sofa, boys sat on the other sofa.

Harry said wondering, "Why do you want us here, Amy?"

"To talk so safely, no one could hear about our secret plan. You know what it is. About Michael and Sharks business."

Katy suddenly said, "Was Sam in the last lesson in school?"

"Of course," Harry replied. "Sam's not here. Michael's not allowed but Sam is allowed, he's all right."

Before everyone could say a word Daniel said, "He lives in the front of my house, I will get him."

Harry said laughing, "Go on, It's near about 1 minute or a seconds."

Soon Daniel arrived at the Sam's house. He picked up Sam. Daniel and Sam arrived at the Daniel's house.

Sam said to Amy, "What are we doing here without our poor friend. Why aren't you letting him come here and play with us?"

Daniel said this time, "Michael's not allowed. Miss Jean told us and we are not playing. We're talking about our secret. It's the safest here, no one's listening here, so, no one's here except Sharks."

Sam said in surprise, "You naughty, silly Dan. There is somebody who is listening your, our, my secret!"

"Who?" Daniel said in surprise, "I have no brothers or sister and my mum and dad is at work."

Sam shouted this time, "Right sitting next you!"

But Daniel still looked puzzled, "What do you mean?"

Amy said laughing, "We didn't tell Sam our important secret, because he was in Miss Jean's office!"

Katy said laughing as well. "Come here Sam, Harry's a Shark, he will find about the Pepsy's secret. Later, Pepsy don't know Harry's our team. Harry will pretend to be Pepsy and tell us! That's our great secret and it's our plan. Grand man indeed, if Mike gets normal again, I will tell him. Soon he will get normal."

Everyone laughed and played until 4 o'clock and all went to their own house happily.

Few weeks later, everyone except Pepsy were waiting for Michael.

At home time, Daniel said, "Shall we go to the Miss Jean's office, I am wondering about Michael." "Good."

Everyone agreed and went to the Miss Jean's office.

Amy spoke, "Good afternoon, Miss Jeansy. We want to know what's going on to Michael, can you tell us?"

Miss Jean said looking at register, "Please call my name properly young lady, Miss Jean, not Miss Jeansy. Miss Jeansy is year 7 teacher in the Wooden Secondary school. And Michael will come by this weekend."

"Yes, Michael's back think how wonderful it will be!"

Everyone shouted in delight.

Next morning Michael come to the school. Katy said when everyone finished cheering him. "We got a great secret, it's very nice plan. It would work nicely, Mike."

Michael seemed very glad. "What is it, tell me."

Sam spoke, "You are polite then you old life, Michael."

Amy said sharply to Sam, "Michael don't want hear that. Anyway, whose house is empty this afternoon."

Daniel said smiling, "Me, me."

Sam spoke. "We will tell you our, my, your secret in Dan's house. It's very grand plan and we don't want spoil it."

By hometime everyone was excited because it was holiday.

Amy said, "Does anyone go holiday?"

Michael replied first, "Our family planned to go to the France but they were too busy because of me and they forgot. We all remembered yesterday that my bigger sisters, Emily and Lusy went for ticket. But there wasn't any ticket with which we can go to the France. So, Fonny, Lusy, Emily, all hates me."

Daniel said, "My mum and dad have to go work so, I'm going to play class because my parent thought I would be boring. I'm going there 4 o'clock to 5 o'clock. There's Olivio, I will play with him."

Then Kate said, "Mum's too tired and Jack is too young for journey so I'm just staying at home."

Sam said, "I'm learning golf at 6 o'clock until 6:30. That's all what I will do everyday."

Amy said at the last, "I'm doing absolutely nothing in the home."

Everyone walked.

Amy whispered to Harry who were trying to be not seen by Michael. "How about you? Harry."

He replied, "Nothing. you know my dad doesn't works except on holidays."

Amy spoke happily, "Good. Nice. Let's make a holiday group at morning 10 o'clock. We shall do it in Daniel's home.

We can't play so much long because Dan and Sam needs to go."

Everyone shouted it was a very really good idea and next day it will be started.

Holiday Club

Saturday morning Shark all come to Daniel's house. But yet they didn't tell Michael their secret, so Harry went to Daniel's bedroom reading a book.

Amy spoke. "Who want to tell our great secret to Michael? Oh right Sam, will you tell it to Michael quietly right?"

Sam said,"Our secret is very grand it probably would work very well. Do you know our new member? Hey, come down."

Michael smiled, "Who is it, come on , Harry Potter, oh yes he is the most clever boy and is it our secret?"

Daniel spoke this time, "No, he's first secret and second's more grand Mike."

Katy said when Harry sat down next to Amy. "Pepsy don't know Harry is a Shark and Harry will pretend to be in Pepsy and he will give us their secret. No one will be hurt because we will know their plan. What do you think about it? Friends?"

"Amazing." said Michael, and they all had tea and went home.

Next day everyone came to Daniel's house.

Sam counted. "Someone's not here. Let me see we got Harry, me, Dan, Katy and Amy. Who's missing?"

Harry counted and checked.

He said, "Michael is missing. I think he forgotten it. Someone had better get him. We can't start it without a person."

Katy said wearing her shoes, "I will get Mike, he lives next road."

Amy asked, "Don't come back without Michael. Do you know which road it is?"

Katy replied going out, "Michael lives in my road. I will come back as soon as possible."

Daniel replied worrying, "Is Michael in trouble? I guess he is. He never never break a promise. I'm quite sure he is in a deep trouble."

Sam said, "Can I have some biscuit? Can you tell me where it is, if you don't mind."

Daniel said still thinking hard, "It's in the fridge. If you want creamy one."

Harry said eating a biscuit, "What sort of trouble you mean?"

Daniel replied, "I told you, Michael never break a promise,

you know the troubles in the street."

"On his way?"

Daniel said looking at Harry, "Yes, or he could have troubles in his home with his parents and not allowed to go anywhere."

Amy said sharply, "Why are you thinking that just Michael will be in the trouble? Do you want that to happen really? He could oversleep or forget it or he got something to ..."

Sam interrupted Amy, "It's delicious, Mmm . . I will beg Mum to buy this one. I'm sick of her chocolate biscuit."

Once more Amy said sharply, " Sam, you are no use, you are just thinking useless thing to us Samuel. Stop eating now, you are not coming here to eat. You are coming here to think."

Then Kate arrived without Michael, her face was full of worries.

She spoke, "I went to Michael's house but there wasn't Michael, there was just Mrs. Park and Emily. I asked where Mike was. But Mrs. Park even didn't know Michael was out. But Emily said every morning he goes to do something in his friend's house. She said Mike went there this morning also."

Kate sighed and continued."On my way back I met Fonny, Lucy and her boyfriend Simone, I asked Fonny and Lucy if they knew where Michael was. But they said that Michael got a club with his friend. I couldn't have more information than that."

Amy said, "Michael might go to Mr. Park's garage to help."

Daniel said, "He lost his way. That's his trouble. We have to find him."

Amy said, "All right, I got a decision. I will go to the garage if Michael's there. Katy you can go with Daniel and, Sam you will have to go with Harry, because Sam and Daniel will surely know their way back to here."

"Why Sam?" Harry asked.

"Sam lives in front of Daniel's house."

They all went to do their job. Amy walked away.

Katy said, "I and Dan will walk up this way. You two can go down that way and search every road."

They all went to do what they had to do.

Amy arrived in garage and saw Michael.

"Hello, Michael, why didn't you come to our club today?"

Michael replied. "I'm very sorry, on my way back I met Dad and had to help him."

"Why?" asked Amy.

"He got another job. He is not mechanic anymore, he is a postman and I can have this garage. I'm helping him clean this up."

Amy ran and shouted, "I will see you, I will get the others."

Easily she found Daniel and Katy, she told them to find Harry and Sam. Amy borrowed Michael's bicycle to go faster. At last they saw Harry and Sam. She told them as well. They all ran to Michael's garage.

They saw Mr. Park. Amy asked, "Can we help you, Mr. Park?"

Michael came out and said, "Of course."

Katy said to Michael, "Is it your garage? Michael, what are you using this garage for?"

He replied painting the wall. "I think I will use this for play-room with friends, specially with 'Shark'."

Sam smiled and gave Katy a broom. "Good boy, Mike, Katy, sweep the floor, if you don't mind."

"Where is Daniel and Amy?"

Sam replied, "Amy's painting the wall and Daniel and Mr. Park is sticking new floor. Oh, we finished sweeping."

Then Daniel and Mr. Park came down.

"Sam, Harry, Can you paint the stair while Dan and I stick the wooden floor. Do you want help Michael painting, Katy?"

"Oh, Yes."

Amy came down. She said, "What can I do for you, now, Mr. Park?"

Mr. Park replied, "Please help Michael painting, Amy."

All of them worked very hard.

Sam said painting the last step. "I finished. Mr. What shall I do for you?"

Mr. Park said proudly, "Oh, many thanks to you. Please clean the living room window. I and Dan finished also. I and Dan will stick new floor in the toilet and clean the toilet." Everyone laughed.

Daniel said, "Oh, What are you laughing about, I like toilet." Everyone laughed. Even more loudly.

Later Amy, Katy, Michael finished.

Katy asked Mr. Park, "What shall we do for you now?"

Mr. Park said, "How about you three cleaning the toilet, whilst I stick the wooden floor in living room with Dan."

Katy said, "Er... yes. Amy and Michael come and clean the toilet." When they saw Katy's red face they all laughed.

When Katy, Michael, Amy finished cleaning toilet, Sam and Harry also finished. So, they all together decorated rooms.

When they finished, Mr. Park spoke. "Thank you very much for your help. Thanks very much. You can play with Michael if you like. It's Michael's. We got 4 bedrooms. But I and Mrs.

Park use one, Lucy use one, Emily uses one. And Michael and Fonny share the room.

Michael can't sleep here but his room it is. Anyway bye, thanks."

Everyone went home happily.

Next morning Sam said, "Bad news everyone, I'm going holiday to Italy with my family and Daniel's family. Sorry, Katy, Mike, Harry, Amy. But My mum won a family ticket 8 people can go. Jeanie thought that Dan's family could go and dad agreed, and Jenny agreed also. So, that's that. So do Dan's mum and dad."

"When are you going?" asked Amy.

"My parents will come here about 30 minute later. So we must prepare our staffs. If my mum and dad comes, we must go."

Michael said, "We can't open the hoilday club but we four could often play in my garage or everyday."

"We had better go now. Bye, Sam and Dan, have a nice holiday." said Harry. All went out.

Katy said, "We could go to Michael's garage and play if Mike don't mind."

I Want Do the Magic !

Ashley is my best friend. We always do something together, but from yesterday he murmured strange things. I was a bit scared about it, but he wasn't practicing other languages. He wasn't learning French or Spanish.

He and I were learning Italian: We started on same time and we were doing exactly same level.

Often I tried to hear what he is saying. It was strange language I never heard!

And I agree to ask him bravely! and and an and

it wa was so so fu fun funny.

Ha ha ha. I can't even say word when I think it.

Can you guess what he said?

He read Harry Potter and he he he wan wanted do do Ma Ma gic Magic and it was Magic MURMURING!

A Lucky Cap

One day Nicholas was reading he heard footsteps. His mum Mrs. Novan came in to Nicholas's bedroom.

She said to Nicholas, "Nicholas, I'm going to shopping centre with your sister Rebecca. Do you want to go also?"

Nicholas thought hard and said, "Oh, I will go with you, Mum."

They all went in to the car. Later they arrived. Rebecca said, "Mummy, Can I choose something I want? Please."

Mrs. Novan said, "I'll tell you later Rebecca. Get out the car first you two."

They all went out Mrs. Novan locked the car door. Rebecca asked again, "Can I? Mummy, Please."

Her mum said, "Oh, Go on then, just one, Rebecca." Nicholas said, "Mum can I?"

She said, "Oh, of course son. If I said 'Rebecca can' 'you can', all right?"

Nicholas nodded, he said, "Mum, come in here. I will look around here if there's something I want."

So, they all went in. The shop was full of hats, caps, shoes and bags.

Later he said loudly, "Mum, I want this cap, come here Mum."

Mrs. Novan replied, "Come here, I lined up to pay for Rebecca's bag."

Nicholas ran to his mum. When they all paid, they went to top of the shopping centre and bought the things Mrs. Novan need. Then they went home.

Nicholas was very proud of his new cap and wanted to show it to his friend Gary. So he went to Gary's house. When he arrived, he knocked the door. Gary's mum Mrs. Blackson opened the door.

Nicholas said, "Mrs. Blackson, Can I go in to your house to see Gary for about 20 minutes?"

Mrs. Blackson replied, "Of course, come in dear." Nicholas went in to Gary's bedroom.

"Hi, Gary. I got my new cap, look at it."

Gary said still looking at the cap, "Wow, it's amazing, wonderful. I want have that, that's my first wish now."

Nicholas smiled. They played for a bit and Nicholas went home.

Next morning Nicholas said to his mum, "Mum , Can I go to walk with my new cap?"

"Yes," said his mum.

So, Nicholas went for a walk. It was very windy day. On his way the wind blew terribly.

And Oh ! dear. Nicholas's cap blew away.

Nicholas forgot all about the walk and searched every-where. About an hour later Nicholas went home without his new cap. He was very sad about it. When he told his mum about it, Rebecca and his mum laughed and Rebecca gave his new cap and said, "When I went to park to get you for break-fast I found your cap. You must say 'Thank you' to me, if it wasn't me, you have lost the cap."

So, Nicholas said, "Thank you" to his sister.

And because of this, Nicholas never wore hats or caps and never bought those.

Silly Jenny Curve

"Jenny, please quickly go to Mr. Smith's shop and buy a biscuit and a carrot and two cokes. Is it okay?" asked Jenny's mum.

It wasn't OK but Jenny nodded.

"Good girl. Do you want me to write down what we need?" asked Jenny's mum, Mrs. Curve.

"No, thank you." She then went to her own little bedroom and got her purse. She went down.

"Mummy, money."

"Right, Jen, 2 pounds would be enough, are you sure that you can remember the thing I need for meeting with Miss Menny?"

Jenny wore her shoes.

"I'm positive I can remember them, Mum. An hour later Miss Menny comes, doesn't she?"

"yes."

"So, I've got enough time. All right. I got purse. And Bye, Mummy. I will back as soon as possible."

Jenny went towards the shop. It was quite far away. The quickest way to get to Mr. Smith's shop was to go through the park. So, Jenny went to the park. She ran off, because she wanted to see Miss Menny.

She loved Miss Menny. Miss Menny was nursery teacher. But now Jenny was in year two. She stopped running. She was exhausted.

At last, she came to the shop. She searched for her pocket but the purse was gone.

"Can you turn the lights on, Mrs. Smith? So I can find my purse."

Mrs. Smith did what Jenny wanted but the purse wasn't there.

"Oh I see, I think I dropped it in the park when I was running."

And it was. So she went back to the shop.

But Dear Me!!

Jenny forgot to buy what.

So she just thought what it was.

Her guess was wrong.

"Mrs. Smith, can I have two cakes and biscuit please?"

She missed the carrot and she said cake instead of coke.

She happily went home.

When she arrived, her mother was busy cooking.

"Oh good girl Jenny. Have you got all the thing I said?"

She looked in the bag.

"Silly girl, I said that you should buy two cokes and carrot and biscuit. You got biscuit. You missed carrot out and you bought cakes instead of cokes!" said Mrs. Curve. She looked angry.

"I have to cook other things. For your punishment, you can't see Miss Menny. You got to stay in your bedroom without a word."

Jenny was really sad but she said nothing and went to bedroom as her mum said.

Because it was her fault.

Aeroplane

Billy : Good Morning, Sian!

Sian : Good Morning.

Billy : Let's go to Libary.

Sian : OK. Are we going to walk all the way to the Libary?

Billy : Oh dear, I didn't think of that. If we are to walk, it's too far away from here. How about riding a bike?

Sian : No way!

Billy : Why not?

Sian : Because I haven't got a bike except that old bike. It doesn't work anymore.

Billy : You can ride on my bike with me.

Sian : Never!

Billy : Oh fine!! We will walk all right?

Sian : Good.

Billy : Sian, Did you ever get in to the plane?

Sian : Lots of time. It's really fun you know, flying in the aeroplane like birds I always wanted to.

Billy : Shut up. I never got in to the aeroplane. I really want to, but our family is so many. Grandma, Grandpa, mum and dad, Katy, Laura, me, Beccy, Sam and baby Jack.

We can't manage them all we haven't got enough money for all of them.

Sian : Poor Billy.

Billy : Hey, How about making my own aeroplane?

Sian : Ha Ha Ha. With paper aeroplane? You're mad.

Billy : I'm not joking, it's real.

Sian : With paper aeroplane?

You Silly Billy.

Billy : I will make real one.

Sian : But how? Billy the Silly, watch where you're going.

We're there.

Billy : I will find out in the book.

Sian : So, come in to the Libary Billy Sandol.

Billy : I am!!!

Sian and Billy went in to the Libary.

In the Libary

Sian : Billy, Here's lot's of books about aeroplane. Here!!

Billy : Coming! Where are you?

Sian : Just near the toddlers books. Hey just come where fiction books are. Then you'll able to find me! Hurry!

Billy found Sian. He started reading books.

Billy : Not this nor this, No, No, No, No.
Exactly. This is exactly the book I need. Sian, I found the book I want. Have you finished?

Sian : Yes, we go.

So, Billy and Sian went to the park with their books. Billy called his uncle Paul. Uncle Paul helped Billy and Sian for weeks to make their aeroplane.

Billy : Wow, It's finishing a proper aeroplane! I'm going off to China with my family and uncle Paul's family and of course your family Sian.

Sian : Thank you very much Billy for inviting me wee hee! My mum will be ever so happy to go to the China. So will my Dad!

Billy : Can you imagine how be my mum will! She really wanted to go on a holiday.

I can't wait to see Laura's shocked face and Sam and

Beccy's exciting face!

I'm ever so happy.

Sian : I'm ever so happy too. Going China!

I'm really looking forward.

Billy : But we're off tonight!

Sian : Let's calm down a bit Billy.

And How shall we call our aeroplane?

Billy : How about BillSiPaulan.

Sian : What?

Billy : BillSiPaulan.

Sian : Bill saying what? Are you speaking Chinese?

Billy : I'm not. BillSiPaulan is special name made up with

Billy, Sian and Paul together.

Sian : Oh, I see Bill Paul Sian . Have I got it , right?

Billy : No, BillSiPaulan.

Sian : Right, BillSiPaulan. Is that right?

Billy : That's it, tell your parents. I'll tell my parents and

uncle Paul. See you!

Billy and Sian went home happily. That night they all went

to China and lived happily after.

The Exciting Holiday

I was so excited. Me, Mum, Dad, big trouble, my big brother Matthew and my little sister Elisa (Ellie), We were going to Switzerland for a whole week to ski. The best thing was no school!(Winter vacation!!!)

In 3 days we were going. Mum and Dad had all their ski stuff. But I, Matthew didn't. Dad said we were going to get them when we get there. Of course Ellie didn't have any of the ski stuff. She won't be able to ski anyway. She's still a baby. Screaming all the time is a lot better than your big brother annoying you.

Dony, Matthew's mate was supposed to go with us and we had five seats ordered in the plane. We are not rich by the way.

More like poor in a way but we ordered 5 seats instead of 4 because it was cheaper.(Ellie doesn't need a seat)

Dony brought the news a day ago that he couldn't come because he was going on holiday with his own family to Spain. Dony went home after tea. Matthew started moaning and groaning and kicked everything he saw in sight and also kicked me.

"Mum, Can I bring my friend to." I asked but I was interrupted by rude one.

"Don't you think about that, Miss Smarty Pants. I'm not having another girl spoiling my holiday! And, Miss Goody-Goody, for your extra information Lyce is coming filling in the gap." The stupid one said in a sly voice.

"No way, you greedy one! You've lost your chance now! I'm taking one of my friend. So there, ha ha!" I started backing away and ran. I knew when to run. And yes sure enough Matthew started chasing me round the kitchen. Ha ha! I'm the smart one!

"Stop it, both of you. You'll wake Elisa up. You're like 3 year olds you are. Don't call your friends names Matthew. No wonder Matthew, why Harry doesn't like you, calling each other names. You do know how sensible Harry is." Mum shouted.

"I did not call any of my friends any names!" the ugly one said pulling a face.

"Oh, yes you did. You called Jake Lyce. Don't lie!" I joined in. The smart one did.

"Both of you quiet." Mum snapped.

"Well anyway Mum can my friend come with me?" I said

looking at Mum really sweetly.

"Mum can I bring Jake?" Matthew tried to copy me but he only looked like a dog begging for some food.

"Well, Matthew I think Grace is right this time."

"So does that mean I can bring my friend?" I exclaimed my eyes twinkling of excitement.

"That's the only meaning Grace!"

Ellie started yelling and Mum went into the living room to see what was the matter.

"But Mum, that's not." Matthew began.

"No arguing and I think it is fair." Mum growled back. Matthew winged as loudly as he could but that was no use. I was so excited I could hardly stand still.

"Mum! Can I go round to Andrea's? And then maybe to Hannah's place! I mean her grandpa and ma's place?" I shouted. I was going to ask Andrea (Andy) first then Hannah. They were my two best friends. I had more friends but I wanted to ask Andy or Hannah first.

"Yes but be back by dinner!" Mum yelled back.

The fresh evening air was lovely. I ran all the way to the other side of the town to Andy's house. I rang the doorbell and Andy's mum answered.

"Hello? Can I help you?" she said.

"Um... I'm Grace. Is Andy I mean Andrea home?"

"Oh, hello Grace. The doors open. Do come in, sugar."

Andrea came rushing down the stairs.

"Oooh, Hiya Grace. Hey, do you want to taste some of most delicious and ridiculous flavoured ice cream? I invented it!" Andy yelled excitedly.

"Oh sure! What flavour is it ?"

"It's like Love and Hate. Some people love it and some people think it's yuck yuck yuck."

"What ingredients?" I asked suspiciously.

"You wouldn't want it if I read the recipe out to you." Andy giggled.

"No problem!" I smiled. Andy is a great fun.

"Mixed egg yolks, natural honey and chocolate mousse and some raspberry yogurts." she read it out quietly.

"Gone off it already! Mixed egg yolks! Not my taste of delicious ice cream!" I said backing away.

"I told you, you would think it was disgusting! But do taste a little bit please. I'll share a secret with you," Andy said smiling.

She knew I'd go for it. I loved secrets. And I kept them really well so I knew nearly everybody's secrets.

"OK. Gimme a little." I settled myself down at the table.

Andy gave me a little bit. She settled opposite me and ate some ice cream too.

"Like it?" she said with her mouth full of egg-yolk flavoured ice cream.

"Mmm... Not bad for the first invention. Taste quite good actually. Yum, yum, yum."

Andy smiled. She always got it her way.

"Worked on ya!" Andy exclaimed.

"What's your secret?" I whispered.

"Only telling if you won't tell anybody," she said.

"Cross my heart and hope to die," I said quickly.

"OK. This flavour can be horrible when you've had some nice chocolate ice cream from Cath's chip shop. Well this stupid boyfriend of Josie's (Andy's big sister) Mark is really getting on my nerves. Although I'm going to give Josie the chocolate and strawberry. I'm going to give Mark yolk flavoured one. How does that sound to you?"

Andy asked pouring some Pepsi into two glass.

"Sounds great clever one," I said.

We usually had dinner at six and it was five. I had to get going.

"You going anywhere over the winter holidays?" I asked her.

She didn't hear me because she turned on the TV.

"Hey, Grace ! Do you wanna see my ice cream maker? Well, Max's (Andy's big brother) but he's gone out so it's mine!" Andy whispered in a quiet voice.

"And maybe we could get ready for the trick!"

"Cool!!!" That moment I forgot everything about my holiday.

We went up to Andy's room. There was the ice cream maker tucked in carefully by a blanket.

"So, let's get down to business!" Andy shouted.

"What color was my ice cream, Grace ?"

"Chocolaty brown with some yellow and pinky bits," I replied.

"Oka!! (This is a made up word. Andy always uses this word when she's made a decision or that kind of thing) I've get an idea. We'll make for Josie strawberry, chocolate flavour. Grace could you make ice creams for Josie while I get some tea ready for them two and some ice cream for Mark."

She said winking. She went down. And I pressed strawberry and chocolate and pressed start. When I had bowlful I carried it down to Andy. And I had still forgotten, completely forgotten about my holiday.

Josie and Mark came in about 5 minutes later. Me and Andy

had everything set up. We had five pieces of jam and buttered toast. 2 glass of Pepsi two chocolate bars and of course our two different flavoured ice cream.

"Oh hello Grace. This is Mark. Mark, this is my sister Andy's friend Grace," Josie said smiling.

"Oh hello sister and Mark!" Andy said very sweetly.

"I and Grace have made some tea for you. Do you like jam and butter toast, Mark?"

"Oooh, I simply love them!" Mark exclaimed.

"Pepsi?" I asked and Andy joined in as well.

"Sure," Mark replied.

We all went in to the dining room where the tea was ready.

"Very rare." Josie muttered. But sat down and both of them began to eat as if they'd never seen food before. I and Andy ate 2 pieces of toast. When they'd nearly finished their tea, Andy got going.

"Um... Wanna some ice creams?" Andy asked.

Josie stared suspiciously.

"Has the toasts been on the floor or have you licked it or is there something wrong with it?" She asked.

"Apparently none of them is true," I replied.

"Ok. What about the Pepsis? Did you spit in them?" Josie said.

"Or pour dog wee in it !" Andy whispered.

Mark must have caught some few words like pour dog wee. He went pale green and said Excuse me and went to the loo.

"Ice creams?" I asked but Josie ignored me.

"Something wrong with something. Unusual to see you two actually preparing tea for someone else." She said pushing all the thing (e.g plates, cups...) away from her. Andy pushed them back.

"Grace loves cooking actually but her mum doesn't let her so I thought it would be a chance for her to make tea," Andy said looking so innocent.

"I do all the co..." I began.

"Cleaning but she can't do cooking." Andy gave me a kick.

"Yeah!" I muttered.

Josie nodded.

"Okay. Fine enough," Josie muttered unsurely.

"Sorry about that. Um. What time is it? Better be going." he murmured and gave Josie a fake smile.

"It's only 10 to 6. I thought you wanted to stay for dinner?" Josie said.

"Naah, it's OK. I feel a bit sick and we've got homework to do." Mark said heading for the door.

"Yeah! Forgot about it! Bye! See you at school!" Josie said.

"No, No! Mark! You should taste this ice cream. We made it especially for you. Show us some respect, Uh? Huh!" Andy said beggingly. In the end Mark said, 'Yes'. Andy can be a right pest in the neck. But good one Andy!

Josie began to eat the ice cream immediately.

"Why has Mark got yellow bits and I haven't?" Josie asked suspiciously.

"Only, er ... e . ," I began than realised the trick in time.

"It's soft caramel flavour."

"Only for guests," I added. Andy smiled pleasingly.

"Oh." Josie said without noticing that Mark was pale green and looked as though he was going to be sick any minute. Mark went to the toilet once again but he went home straight-away.

In Andy's room we giggled for a bit then Andy's mum called me.

"It's from your mum, Grace," she said holding out the phone to me.

Then I realised it was six.

"Grace !" my mum bellowed angrily.

"Uh ... yes?" I said very nervously.

"It's six. We're waiting for you to have dinner. I told you to come back home by six. So come back home now ! Clear?"

"Yep. Give me 5 min," I replied. It's not worth arguing with my mum.

Before I put the phone down. Andy's mum took the phone and spoke.

"Hello, how are you doing? I am Andrea's mum."

"Oh, hi! I'm OK, thanks, What about you?"

"Just a bit busy, sorting out bits and bobs for winter holiday." Andy's mum, Mrs. Jeff.

"Me too," Mum replied.

"Oh, Mrs. Hunt, Grace could have dinner with us."

"No, don't bother."

"Yeah! Go on, Mrs. Hunt! Please..." Andrea squealed.

"Okay then ... Be back by 8!" My mum said.

"Yes ~ ~!" We squealed.

Then a thought passed me. The winter holiday !!

"Andy, are you going anywhere this winter?"

"Yeah! I'm going to Florida!"

"Cool!" I said, but I didn't really mean it. I was really looking forward to going to Switzerland with Andy. But I thought I still had Hannah.

We were listening to Britney Spears' music (stole it from Josie) when Mrs. Jeff called us.

"Dinners ready!!"

We ate dinner talking about schools and kids in school. It was 6:40 when we finished dinner. So I thought I'd better go to Hannah's before 7. So I told Andy that I had to pop into Hannah's to ask something. Andy looked disappointed but she let me go.

Hannah's was not far away. It was 8 minutes walk. When I arrived at Hannah's home, I was very nervous. Because her gran is really strict about everything. But I'm really a nice lady, really I am.

Ding-dong-ding-dong. I pressed the bell.

"Who's there?" Hannah's gran's sharp voice broke the peace in the street.

"Sorry to bother you, but I'm Hannah's friend Grace. I've come here to ask something to Hannah."

I said very nervously and added, "if possible"

"You may come in."

Hannah's grandparent's house is enormous, although Hannah's house is just a flat. Hannah came running out opening the front gates.

"Hi , Grace!! What's the business? I thought you were on holiday !!"

"Not yet. I'm leaving the day after tomorrow, at early morning."

"Oh, you're really lucky. I heard you were going to Switzerland?"

I nodded. We stepped into the house. I said 'hello' to Hannah's grandparents and went running into her room. (She's got a room equipped with everything, even though she doesn't sleep everyday here. But she stays here most of the day.)

"Hey, Hannah, you want to go on a vocation."

"There's nothing to say about that. Bet, you are going there to ski?"

"Sure. You can come with me on vacation, if you want."

"Oh, I would love to... But everything will be so complicating. Getting the airplane ticket. May be the ticket could be all sold out. The only thing that I have is skiing stuff."

"Hey, don't worry about anything! All ready...

We've got an extra ticket for you."

"Really thanks! I'm gonna ask my gran about this!"

She went scurrying out. She added. "You can play computer games while I'm downstairs."

I switched on the computer games. Hannh's computer is really cool. The window is XP. So, it works really fast. I played action games.

After several minutes Hannah came up the stairs. Her face

92

was screwed up. She looked like as if she would cry.

"My grandma said I'm talking nonsense~she does not belive me. I begged her I really wanted to have a vacation. Grace, can you explain to my grandparents? Please~ There's no need to be nervous to them~."

"Er~ But..."

"Please do not hesitate... I really want to have a vacation... Well~ Actually I didn't even imagine going on a vacation before you came... Mum and dad working all day all night! Their boss doesn't want them to have even one day vacation! Gosh~ Grace you just have to go ! You must be responsible for making me excited ~"

Hannah was really exhausted. I bet she really wanted to go on a vacation. Her mum and dad works every day, even Sundays, all day long. Although Hannah's grandparents are London's one of the richest people, Hannah's mum and dad were not very well living family. Hannah rarely saw her parents. The only day she could be with her parents were national holiday such Christmas.

"But I bet they will think I'm really really rude~ ."

"But~"

"I will give it a go."

"Oh~ Thank you~"

I was very nervous actually. Hannah's grandpa (Mr. Long-heck) was watching the telly and her grandma was reading a magazine.

"Er... Excuse me. Mrs. and Mr. Longheck... Could Hannah go on a holiday with our family?" I spoke.

Mr. and Mrs. Longheck stared at me they made faces as if they couldn't understand what I was saying.

"I'm sorry dear. Hannah's mother and father wouldn't want to spend money to send their daughter on a holiday..."

Her grandma snapped sharply. Then she spoke under her breath. She spoke loud enough as if she wanted me to hear.

"Only if my son hadn't married that stupid woman!!! Oh my poor son~ He has to work work work~ If he had married someone else he would be richer at least not so poor! He could go on holidays~.

Poor Hannah~ She has met a wrong mother~ Why, oh, why did Richard (Hannah's dad) marry somebody who hasn't got a penny and all she has is a £1(1pound) in total~. That women is a~" Mrs. Longheck's voice go louder by rage. Mr. Longheck stopped her before she could say any more.

Hannah was really droopy.

I didn't know what to say. I just wanted to go home. But I thought of Hannah and opened my mouth.

"But please. I am not requiring you any money but just Hannah and her skiing stuff~ . You see our family is 5. But my sister is a baby so she does not need a seat. The airplane company said they prepare special baby seat. We reserved 4 seats but reserving 5 seats was a little bit more cheaper. So, you don't need to spend any money~ Please... It will be good if somebody sat on the spare seat than nobody sitting there..."

Mr. and Mrs. Longheck looked at each other. There were peace for several minutes.

"Okay, Let's let Hannah go!" Mrs. Longheck broke the silence.

"But~ Wouldn't we need to ask her mum or her dad?" Mr. Longheck spoke out carefully.

"They are not worthy enough to decide what Hannah should do and should not do," She said sharply.

She turned her body around to me and spoke.

"Oh and Grace dear. Thank you for inviting Hannah. When are you leaving?"

"Er... the day after tomorrow.. so it's Friday. (Today was Wednesday) But Hannah should come to our house by 5 am. The planes leaving at 7:30 am. Hannah just have to bring her skiing stuff and some pocket money if necessary!!" I smiled.

I looked up accidentally, and there was a clock ticking and

tocking.

It was pointing 8:20 ! Oh no~ Mum would be mad at me.

I stood up immediately and said, "I'm supposed to be back by 8. I'd better go! Hannah, Friday, by 5!! And goodbye everybody ~"

I ran as far as my body could go. It was usually 15 minute's walk, but I arrived there in 8 minutes. I was so exhausted. I shut the door really loudly. At that moment Ellie started crying. 'I hate Ellie.' I thought.

Mum came out with a disgusted face. "Grace, be graceful. You really do sometimes drive me total nuts ! It's 8:30 now. You have been playing outside all day. And now, I could have let you go if you hadn't woken up Ellie. She hasn't got a proper sleep because of you and Matthew. She has woken up at least 5 times today !"

"I'm really sorry, mum. I couldn't help it."

I went to my room very quickly.

It was a busy day today. I was very proud.

However, the day after tomorrow will be a exciting holiday.

The Story of Linny

Zoe's Broken Present

CHAPTER 1

"No, you did it," cried Melly.

"No, Billy did," yelled Sandy.

"No, William did it," shouted Billy.

"Melly, you did it liar," cried William.

I, Linny was watching the argument between the four kids. Sandy was my friend and I was waiting for her actually. I was waiting for the argument to end.

I waited for a while but argument (about someone who has broken Zoe's birthday present) did not end and I was bored and also could not bear hearing the argument anymore.

I just wanted to shout at them and I did,

"Hey, could you stop that! No one did it. Somebody in Zoe's class did it because it was there."

"But Zoe's really upset about it," said Melly.

"But, Billy or you, or Sandy or William did not do it. None of your business I say."

"It's my business," cried Melly again.

"I know what !"said Billy suddenly. "It's you Linny. You broken it and you're trying to change to conversation."

I was not the one who did it. I liked Zoe really much. I wanted to say something but I didn't. I did not want to speak. I just ran away from four of them and sat on the corner quietly. I pretended I was not seeing four of them but really I was looking at them. They were starting the argument. That meant now they did not think I have broken Zoe's present.

When I looked up to four of them again, Sandy was running towards me. She sat next to me.

"You all right, Linny?" asked Sandy.

"I think so," replied I.

I was a bit embarrassed and I couldn't see her face straight. I stared down the floor.

"Tell me the truth. Who do you think has broken Zoe's present? I am certain you didn't do it Linny and also me. Because we spent all the morning in the library," said Sandy.

She looked so calm not like the others.

"It's just my guess I think it's Melly because she is half so excited and half she is pretending to be sad. How about you?"

Melly really was so excited. I could guess with just her voice.

"I think it's Billy. He keeps saying silly things. He just says 'It's Sandy.' Then if somebody says Melly is, he says 'It's Melly.' and if somebody says it's William, he agrees again or if someone says it's Billy, his face goes red and shouts really loudly like 'No, you're' or 'I'm not' and things like that."

It might be Billy I thought.

CHAPTER 2

Next morning, of course I came to the school. Nothing was found out yet. Teachers tried hard too, but nothing happened.

Even my teacher Mrs. Maloney said to us,

"If someone tells me who has broken Zoe's present, I promise I will give you a sweet."

But no one was found out. But I did in the afternoon. In the afternoon at break time, Sandy and I stayed inside in the changing room where all the bags were. Melly and Pop (her real name is Elizabeth) was also there. But Pop went out but Melly stayed. Sandy went to the toilet and I read a book. I sometimes looked at Melly. When second time I looked at her, she took my hairband from my bag. I chased after her. Something dropped out her pocked. It was Zoe's piece of her present. I will get the hairband later. I took the piece. I ran to Mrs. Maloney who was coming back to classroom. The bell rang. Sandy came out and she followed me. I went in to the classroom.

I was really exhausted. "Mrs. Maloney, I found out who has broken Zoe's present. It's Melly." And I told her what had happened.

Mrs. Maloney looked surprised. Sandy looked surprised as well.

"How do you know, Linny?" asked Mrs. Maloney.

"Look at this piece, Mrs."

Everyone came in.

"Right, Melly come here," She showed the piece. Everyone looked surprised.

"Who found it, Mrs. Maloney?" asked Sam.

"Linny did, well done." Everyone clapped.

"Linny, come here, here's your sweet. Now could you go to Head Master's office with the piece and of course with Melly. Tell him what had happened. Melly, give the hairband back to Linny."

And after that I was the Hero.

The Revenges Made from an Argument

CHAPTER 1

I, Linny sat on a shade. There was an argument between Billy and Pop. It was nothing to do with me, of course. But Sandy my friend is interested in all the arguments and was giggling with Melly. Melly was friend of Pop.

Suddenly I heard Sandy saying,

"Pop, you're a complete liar."

"Sandy, shut up. Billy is a liar." Melly was nearly shouting.

"No thanks, Mel," said Sandy.

"You're stupid Sandy. I would probably say to you, you're ugly." said Melly who always used rude words first.

"I'm not and I hate you, silly. Dare you to say I'm ugly. I hate you, I repeat. Huh!" And Sandy come to me.

I was quite worried if something would happen, but nothing did.

CHAPTER 2

Next day I came to school in the afternoon. Because I had to go to the dentist. When I came I found Sandy inside in the changing room. She looked really frightened.

"What's the matter, Sandy? You look so worried." I asked her.

"I am." She replied.

Her face was red. She looked if she was trying hard not to cry.

"Why?" said I.

"Somebody tore my homework into the pieces. What's more important is that some piece are missing."

Lucy came in. She asked the same question as I did.

"What's the matter, Linny and Sandy? Can I help you?"

I looked at Sandy. She looked as if she could not speak, so I spoke.

"Somebody tore out Sandy's homework. We could stick it together if any piece wasn't missing, but few of them is missing and Sandy and me don't know who done it."

"I think I could help you." said Lucy hopefully.

CHAPTER 3

"I'm really certain that Melly did it. I saw her." She went to the Melly's bag. She searched something.

"Here we're. It's the basis." said Lucy.

It was a piece of paper. A piece of homework.

"I'll revenge you back, Melly. I'm afraid I need a lie. Both of you, don't tell anybody about it specially to Mrs. Maloney or I'll revenge back to you instead of Melly," said Sandy angrily.

Girls and boys came in.

I said, "It must be the end of the play."

Lucy, Sandy and I went in to the classroom.

CHAPTER 4

"Right kids, sit down and read quietly while I check the homework," said Mrs. Maloney.

She all looked round the class.

I thought everyone had their homework except Sandy. At last she came to me, she collected my homework then she went to Sandy who was sitting next to me.

"San, (Mrs. Maloney calls Sandy as San but Sandy doesn't mind) Where's your homework?"

"I had done my homework then I putted it in the table. My brother, Selfroy saw it then he carried it to his room. And later when mum brought my brother's juice, he spilled the juice over my homework, then it got tore out and it's wet. The piece are missing. Could you give me another sheet, Mrs. Maloney." Sandy whispered so quietly that Mrs. Maloney hardly could hear.

"Right, San. You must bring it tomorrow if I give you a new sheet, Promise?" She(Mrs. Maloney) said.

"Promise. Mrs. Maloney," replied Sandy.

Mrs. Maloney gave her a new sheet. About 30 minute later the bell rang for break.

CHAPTER 5

Once again me and Sandy went to changing room. Sandy wanted a private talk with me. Actually the changing room was not private place after all. People kept coming for drinks and put off their coats mostly. So, Sandy and me had to find another private place.

At last we found it. It was in the library at the corner there was a space and two chairs.

It was a perfect place for a private talk. We chose any book we pretended we were reading but we wasn't. Sandy and I was whispering. No one noticed.

"You're my best friend. Agree?" asked Sandy.

"Positive," I said. I had to be friend with her because really, girls did not like me because I was quiet. If I did not want to play with Sandy, I had no friends. Lucy could be but now she already had her best friend, Karren.

"Do you promise to keep this secret forever?"

"Promise," I said.

She began.

CHAPTER 6

"Now I will revenge back to her, you see. What I will do is tore something out or I'll damage her things. Agree?"

I was not at all pleased with her idea. There would be more trouble I thought but I just nodded like a fool. Sandy walked I followed her.

"Lin, go to changing room and see if someone's there,"said Sandy.

I did not like the way she spoke.

"Sandy could you not call me Lin and if you ask for something could you speak politely?" I said.

It was first time that I spoke to her like that.

"Oh right Linny, Could you please go to the changing room and see if someone's there?"

She looked quite angry but I didn't care.

I did not like people who was not polite when they asked something to other people. And I did not liked to be friend who did not take care of other people.

"All right. I will. I'll come back in a minute." I went in there was no one.

CHAPTER 7

I went back to Sandy.

"There's no one there," I said.

"Are you sure?" asked Sandy.

"Sure."

"Are you positive?"

"No," I said. Because if someone was there, it was my fault and I did not wanted to be blamed by Sandy.

"Then what did you do when you went in?"

Once more I was angry the way she spoke.

"Don't speak to me like that. I don't like people who doesn't take care about anything."

Sandy walked away she looked really angry this time. So, I tried to go to library to spend my time but the bell rang and I went to classroom.

CHAPTER 8

"Right in English you had a sheet of paper that needed to be done. I'll go round and collect in, if you haven't I would like the reason," said Mrs. Maloney.

She started from our table. Everyone had their homework except Melly.

I knew the reason. Sandy did it.

I don't know but I think like Sandy have done. She wanted to revenge back to Sandy. So she, too used a lie.

"I'm sorry, Mrs. Maloney," said Melly.

"I would like the reason young lady, Why?" asked Mrs. Maloney firmly.

"Because last night straight after school, we went to park and I lost my homework."

"So what Melanie?(Melly's real name was Melanie)"

"Could you give me another sheet of paper?"

"Please. Say politely. Say it again and promise me like San did."

"Please could you give me another sheet Mrs. Maloney if you do I promise I will bring it tomorrow."

Mrs. Maloney gave Melly new sheet then our class started the lesson. It was about making up our own characters. Easy-Peasy.

When Mrs. Maloney was about to explain the next activity the bell rang and all of us went out. I had nothing to do, because I had no friends now so, I thought I will go to the library and sit in the corner and think or read. So, I went to library. Lucy was sitting there. I sat next to her.

Lucy spoke to me first.

"Hiya! Why aren't you playing with San?"

"Why aren't you?"

I did not like to answer first.

"Because I fought with her really. She keeps calling me rude names like froggy Lucy so I said to Karren doggy Karren then she got angry and walked away. How about you?"

"At the play after lunch, I and Sandy stayed inside. It's not important thing but she just cares about her. She's been rude, I didn't like her at that moment. It was not me who walked away she walked away."

"I see," said Lucy.

The bell rang. Lucy and I ran to classroom. Everyone was

already there except Mrs. Maloney.

CHAPTER 9

William came to me and Sandy.

"Okay listen to me especially, you Sandy. When I was in the changing room I saw Melly breaking your mug."

"I know that, Willy. Mrs. Maloney know that I'm angry, Mrs. Maloney is angry. Don't even talk about it, Willy."

I knew Sandy was lying. Mrs. Maloney came in.

"Right kids. This is art. Have you got an object?" She went around the room. She came to our table she checked Rosie and Billy. She checked me.

"Where is your's San?"

Sandy showed Mrs. Maloney broken pieces.

"Why is it broken, young lady? I'm really cross with you today."

Very quietly Sandy spoke. "Mrs. Maloney, I broken it in the morning, I threw my bag in the playground it must be that. I'm sorry. I could draw an apple which I got them for my lunch."

Mrs. Maloney looked really angry.

"Sandy, what a silly girl you're, you can't draw broken pieces so oh, go on quickly get your apple. Hurry up! San."

When Sandy got her apple, Mrs. Maloney explained us what to do then we started sketching.

The bell rang. It meant it was home time.

"Pack your thing and ready to go kids and off you go."

I got really worried things were getting really worse. I had to stop it. I thought for a moment. No idea except telling Mrs. Maloney. I walked home thinking hard.

CHAPTER 10

It was Friday morning. It was raining. I did not like raining. But today I liked raining it was suitable for my plan. I was not sure the plan would work but I just wanted to let it go.

At break time I checked if there was anyone in the changing room.

No one. It's perfect, I thought. I searched the Melly's bag. There was a piece of paper. I tore it out in to pieces. Then I searched Sandy's bag. Good. There was a sheet as well I tore it out too. Then quickly I went in to the classroom.

Both of them was in the classroom. The next thing I had to do was part of a plan which was really important. If I hadn't got this right, things would go worse. I went to Harries (He was moving school but I was not certain.)

"Harries!" I called him. Harries looked back to me.

"Bye, bye Linny, I liked you really much. Thanks for all your help."

"What do you mean?" I knew what he meant. He was leaving. But I wanted double check.

"I'm leaving, bye!"

Now I was certain he was leaving. The plan was going on perfectly.

"Bye, good bye!"

Then I came to the classroom. First I went to Melly.

"Melly, I want to have a private talk with you, can I?" I asked her really politely.

"No! yelled Pop.

"Elizabeth ! Elizabeth. (Pop's real name is Elizabeth. Everyone thought Elizabeth was boring name.) ELIZABETH !" Mrs. Maloney shouted.

"Yes, Mrs. Maloney."

"Quiet."

Melly followed me. When me and Melly was outside the class. I said to her quietly.

"Melly, I saw Harries tearing a paper from your bag when he left the school."

"You're lying liar. He is a sensible boy. It's not true, isn't it?" She said so rudely.

"It is true. I never lie. You know that. You trust me. I swear it's true." Well, I didn't want to say 'I swear it's true'. Because it wasn't.

"Sure?"

"Positive."

"Right, I'm going to tell Miss Ellis about it. Come with me if you're OK, Lin." Not polite enough.

"Where's your 'thank you' gone Mel? And where's your 'Please' gone, also my name isn't Lin either." I said quite rudely.

"All right. I don't know the reason why I should say 'thank you' to you. But we haven't got enough time so, Oh! Thank you and please. Would you please come with me to Miss Ellis, Linny?"

I nodded. We easily found Miss Ellis.

Melly said to her.

"Er, Miss Ellis. Can I talk to you for a minute, please?"

CHAPTER 11

"No problem at all girls."

Melly began.

"Um, Recently most of my things got damaged and disappeared and it's Harries who've done it. Linny saw him."

"Oh dear. Harries just left. We can do nothing about it, because Harries is just gone. I'm afraid Melanie. I'm sorry, Yep?"

We nodded and walked to the classroom.

"Miss Ellis is right. We can do nothing about it when Harries is gone," Melly murmured.

The next important plan, if this works out really well,.... it would be great.

CHAPTER 12

"Sandy, Sandy?" I called her.

"What? You silly pig."

I was really angry but I didn't say much thing about her politeness.

"Sandy, Come on cheer up. Please I'm sorry about that. I know I'm always fussy. But can we be friends again, please~"

I said so nicely but Sandy looked still angry and I was getting angry also.

"I really need to tell you something very important. Come on Sandy, it's not like you. You were a cheerful girl that's why everyone likes you. Be back to cheerful girl."

Now, I thought this was enough. If she still looks angry, well I never will be her friend Never Ever.

"All right I'm sorry. Right, what is an important talk then?" She smiled.

"Come out of the classroom. It's well, sort of private talk it is."

We went out of the classroom.

"Well when you were in the classroom, I was in to the changing room. And I saw Harries who left the school tearing your work. I was so shocked that it had been Harries who damaged your stuff," I said so worriedly.

"I'm sure you're not lying so, what was that Lucy had said to us?" said Sandy.

"Well, it was like well sort of lie or like you know she must have been mistaken."

The bell rang.

"Well then I have no reason why I blamed Melly."

After that Melly, Pop, Sandy and I become best friends.

Wasn't that idea best best idea in the world?

Well I thanked Harries and said Sorry to him several times in my mind. (not on the phone!! Never!)

Well I was superhero again.

Wasn't I?

Trouble and Problem Family

It was boiling day but it was quite windy too. Hank was watching Pokemon Character book in his bedroom, he called his twin sister.

"Judy, July, come, quickly."

Instead of Judy and July his mum came in.

"Hank, change your cloth and do it yourself."

Hank went to his mum's bed room, he wore a T-shirt and a jumper and a trouser. His mum who was combing her hair said to Hank, "Hank, this is boiling you don't have to wear a jumper."

But Hank said, "I don't have any clothes to wear mum, if I had many clothes like Judy and July, what would be the problem?"

His mum spoke, "Oh never mind."

When his mum went to the kitchen, Hank called his little sisters.

"Judy, July, for a minute, quick."

July and Judy came in.

Hank continued. "Can't we go to the front garden and play?"

But both of them said nothing.

"Judy, July, why can't we go outside to the front garden and play?" Hank said most softly way.

Hank was a boy who was ever so lonely child and he got angry at any moment and no one wanted to be his friend. So, he always had to play with his sisters, however Judy was really busy child. She was popular and had a lots of friends to play with.

July, she had friends also. She was just a normal child.

Judy replied, "Sorry, Hank, I got a meeting with Hannah, Natalie and another 2 boys. I'm afraid I can't play with you."

July spoke, "I could play with you Hank if you like but are we allowed?"

Judy went out of Hank's room.

I hate Judy, thought Hank, he suddenly remembered July's question.

"Oh of course, I will ask mum."

Both of them went down.

Hank asked, "Mum? Mum?... Mum !"

His mum hurried coming out the kitchen,

"Oh dear Hanky got angry again and yes? Hank." Hank

replied with a angry voice, "Can I go out to the front garden with July?"

His mum said not looking at Hank, "Why not Judy?"

"Judy is stupid. She never listen to her great brother of hers," said Hank.

"Don't say my daughter is stupid, Hank. She got to listen to me not you Hanky," said his mum staring at Hank.

"Mum!... Anyway can I go out side?" cried Hank.

"It is too sunny, put your caps on both of you."

Hank's face was red. He look very angry indeed, he looked like volcano which will erupt soon.

"MUM! Can I go out?"

His mum looked as if she can't bear hearing Hank's shouting and yelling.

She replied, "Erupted, oh dear. Oops, sorry! I forgot. Oh, I mean, oh you shall go out with your caps on July and Handkerchief."

'Oh.. Oh.' July thought Mummy is strange today. Hank will be really really angry as like Mum said he is erupting again.

July was right.

Hank yelled, "Mum, I'm Hank, Hank not Hanky or ... a Handkerchief. You're having fun with me. You're, you were, you say again."

His mum sighed and said again, "You shall go out with your caps on July and Hank."

This time Hank's mum said properly, so July and Hank went to their bedrooms to get their cap.

Hank said, "Aha! I'll put my new caps on."

But however in July's room there was a problem. July was using her room with Judy. Judy was having a cross temper when July came in.

Judy asked, "What trouble, July?"

July replied, "No trouble. Just need my cap."

Judy ran and held July's cap before July.

July thought, Judy was trying to help. She was about to say 'Thank you'.

Judy said, "Sorry July, I need this cap. I got to go."

July said, "Judy, That's my cap. you lost your cap. If I don't wear hat I can't go outside and if I don't go outside I cannot play with poor Hank."

"No way. I need it."

"That's mine. If the owner said you can't use it or you can't do it you got to do what the owner said."

"I don't care about that silly old rule."

"If you don't give that cap right now I will tell Daddy about it or maybe Hank."

Judy laughed she said, "Oh, I don't care. I don't care about everything, do what you like July."

And did July. She went down to see her dad.

He was sitting on a sofa and was watching a TV show.

July said, "Daddy, Judy is being silly and naughty. Sort this problem out, Daddy."

Her dad said not showing any nerve, "July or Judy? Whoever you're I had enough problems."

July tried again, "But Daddy..."

"Shup up July or Judy? Are you Judy? Never mind what ever your name is." interrupted her Dad.

July knew it will be no use.

When she was about to talk about it to her Mum, Hank came down wearing his new cap, he asked July, "July why aren't you wearing the cap, did you changed your mind not to go out?"

"No, I did not. It is the problem with Judy."

Hank knew a lot about Judy, he said to July, "She's having a cross temper isn't she? But what is the problem with Judy in cross temper?"

"She don't give me my cap. She will soon go out wearing my cap, then I cannot go outside. So, I cannot play with you, Hank, do something."

"Handkerchief please get me some tissues."

'Oh Mum' thought July, he was in good temper but you will make him in bad temper.

July was exactly right.

Hank was in really good temper, but again the volcano was about to erupt.

"Mum! You silly, how dare you to call me Handkerchief again, humph! I'm will not get you some tissue like you have said to me, do it yourself."

Oh please Mummy don't erupt the volcano again.. Please say okay or call me for some tissue..Don't have mistake just say okay.

She was really feeling uneasy. But her mum said 'Sorry' and said nothing.

When Hank settled down Hank went in to the Judy and July's room with July. Judy and July must have to do what Hank had said because it was their familie's rule: Wife got to listen to husband. Children got to listen to parents. Younger sister or brother got to listen to older brother or sister.

Hank hated this rule and break the rule but no one cared. But when the others break the rule he really cared about them.

Hank said to Judy, "Naughty girl Judy, fairly you got to listen to great brother."

'Great?' thought Judy. He is stupid not great.

"Give the hat I mean the cap to July. Listen to your older brother, Judy."

Judy could not have any choice. So, she handed July her cap.

July said to Hank, "You're a great brother of mine sir Hank."

Hank smiled.

Judy wanted to say 'Both of you are so stupid especially you Hanky.' but she could not. If she do that, she might be in a big trouble, so, Hank and July came out to the their front garden.

Hank said to July, "Okay, July, Let's go to the back garden and play superman!"

July nodded but she asked herself how do you play superman? So, July decided to ask Hank.

"Hank, I don't know how to play superman."

"It's easy. really simple. You just pretend like superman or superwomen then you ran, it is a race with pretending like a superhero or superwomen or whatever it is," said Hank.

They done once and Hank was really hot with jumpers on. Hank tried to put off his jumper.

A wind blew.

And Oh! no, Hank's cap blew off.

July saw that she held her cap tightly, holding her cap she ran for Hank's cap for her poor brother!

But still Hank did not notice his cap blew off because he was still putting his jumpers off.

The wind continued. July could not see it anymore. She told Hank about it when Hank putted his jumper off. He looked as though he'll erupt again. He ran to the house, July followed.

Hank did not shout at his Mum or Dad, he shouted at July.

"July, You are not my favorite person anymore. You saved your cap but you did not save my new cap. Humph!"

July tried to go up but her feet did not move.

Somehow she felt brave, it is not my fault thought July. I will bear listening to Hank's shouting for a moment. I'll tell him... I'm not his stupid little servant anymore. She thought.

"Hank, this is not my fault but why are you yelling at me? I tell you what Hank. Play with your friends from now on. I'm not playing with you anymore. You get angry so often. You blame other people so often too."

Hank's face was red, he really looked like an volcano.

"Shut up you stupid. I thought you were my best person but you're not. I call you ugly sister. I'll call Judy lazy sister. You're ugly. You're. You are."

"That's enough." A voice called. A little girls voice, not July. It was Judy.

She had came to take July's side.

Hank shouted, "There comes lazy sister. Shut up. None of your business!!"

Both of them went up to their own bedroom.

Hank sat at the top of the stairs, he could hear his sisters chatting and laughing. He wished he had his friends who could play with him. He went to the his bedroom then went to the girl's bedroom.

He shouted. He did not wanted, but his brains said he had to.

"Come here both of you. I beg your pardon."

Both of them looked scared of Hank. They quietly said pardon.

Then their mother called. "Girls and boy, Come down."

Hank zoomed down.

I'm telling you this. It is quite interesting. I'm Hank's cousin Mei. I heard it from my auntie.

I don't know what happened next but I know that Hank recently got married and he is really rich.

SILLY GEORGE

George was typing the E-mail to his best friend Mattew. George was not popular in the class. No one really liked him or cared for him except Mattew. He was trying to write 'I hate Stacie and Luisen.' He wrote 'I hate' then his mother Mrs. Smith called him.

"George, George ! Hello?"

"Yes, mom."

"Come down! Now."

"What for?" asked George.

"We are going to the park."

"Can you wait until I finish this E-mail to Matt?" begged George.

"No, We're waiting for you. Right Now! or you'll have a punishment." His mum Mrs. Smith shouted.

"Why are you in a hurry going to the silly old boring park?" asked George.

"There's lots of funny things to watch and to do. There's lots of event for children as well. George! I repeat. If you don't come down you'll have a punishment, Right Now!!"

George sighed. He wasn't concentrating what he was doing. He clicked send instead of save. He closed the computer. He wore coat and he went down. As soon as George came down his family went out without a word.

In the park they had a fun time. George had amazing time and he all forgot about the letter.

Next day was Monday. He loved schools. He loved Monday much. When he had his breakfast, he walked to the school with his little brother Tomi (Y3) and his little sister Josephine (Y2).

"Jo, Hurry up, Now, Jo! I went to meet Matthew quickly as possible and you're spoiling it! Tommy, ugh!" George cried to his brother and sister who was twisting the stick in a big puddle.

"You're not my mummy, George." said Josephine.

"But I am sort of. Come on Tommy, you're older than Jo." said George impatiently.

"You not a women, silly." said Tommy taking no care of George.

George couldn't bear this anymore, so, he walked away because he knew Josephine and Tom would come if he walked away.

And they did.

When they arrived the bell rang. So, they went into their own classroom. Their teacher was Miss Plunge. But today, they had Mr. Windsor.

After the register Mr. Windsor said.

"I am here to take place of Miss Plunge half the day. Miss Plunge told me, we should do art for our first lesson and PE for the next lesson. Calm down. Yes, Luke."

"What are we doing for our art?" asked Luke.

"I'll tell you in a minute. Be quiet. Olivia."

"He's Oliver." shouted someone.

"Oliver", said Mr. Windsor. He waited for the class to calm down. When the class had calmed down, he spoke.

"Right, listen or you'll never understand what to do. With a partner, you'll be given a piece of paper. I'm going to give you magazines and newspapers. First, you'll have to decide what you are going to make. It needs to be a natural place, OK? Then in magazines or newspapers you got to find any picture of it. Cut it and then stick it. Anyone don't understand what to do? No one. Good. Olivia I mean Oliver give out the glues they are there. Michael give out scissors bottom drawer and Natasha piece of papers here. Naomi and Liam find as many magazines and newspapers and give them out. Thu?"

"Shall we start?" asked Thu.

"Hang on. Everybody into partners. Sebation?"

"Yes, Mr. Windsor," replied Sebation.

"Who's your partner?"

"Liam."

"Okay."

George went to Matthew. They always worked together.

"What shall we do?" asked George because he was sure Matthew was working with him.

"I'm sorry George but I'm working with Andy I'm afraid." And he walked away to Andrew.

George didn't Know what to do so he just went to Mr. Windsor.

"Mr. ." began George.

"Hold on George. Right hands up if you haven't got a partner. Natty."

"She's Lottie." said Vexal.

"What's her proper name?"

"Charlie."

"Okay, Charlie, you haven't got partner, so, hands up," said Mr. Windsor.

"Yes, I have," said Charlie.

"Where?"

"Naomi, Here."

"All right. So it's just Abbey and George. Abigail and George you two can work together."

So they did.

All the day Matthew didn't play with George or work with him.

When he arrived with Josephine and Tom he thought hard why Matthew his best mate didn't like him anymore.

Was it because Andy was more popular in the class or was it Matthew didn't like him anymore? But why?

He suddenly remembered the E-mail !

He had clicked send when he just wrote 'I hate' !!!

Matthew never played with him anymore but it was OK. Because he had a new boy for his friend and he was popular! STEVE!

LUCKY George BUT OF COURSE

S I L L Y G E O R G E!

A Wonderful Dream

Ashley was sitting in his room doing nothing. About an hour later he had to go to piano lesson. His piano teacher was Mr. Longton. He was fat and made lots of fuss. He didn't like children much either.

He was silly too.

Ashley really wanted to discover an island. He thought a bit about the island then he fell asleep. He had a amazing dream. It was about exploring an island.

What happened was this:

One day Ashley had a chance to go on a boat with his uncle Ben. It was fine morning. But when afternoon came the day got bad. The wind blew at first and it got worse. The storm thundered terribly and rain fell peacefully. Uncle Ben's ship broken. Everyone had to swim away. This happened while Ashley was sleeping in the ship so, he floated away and ...

"Ashley, you lazy wake up!" It was his mum.

But Ashley didn't want this wonderful dream to go away so he said nothing and tried to sleep again.

"Ashley Blackson! Wake up or you'll have a punishment. Terrible one."

But Ashley didn't care either he will have a punishment because he really wanted this dream not to go away but sadly the dream was gone away and it never came back.

"Mum!" shouted Ashley in his disappointment.

When he came back from piano lesson he tried to get that dream back, but he never did.

My Easter Holiday

I had a wonderful Easter holiday this year. I went in a package coach trip. I went to loads of countries in Europe. And I want to share the adventures of my Easter holiday with you.

At about 5 or 4 am in midnight on Good Friday our family had to leave Leek to set off to London. Before I didn't know what Good Friday actually was. I thought it was Good Friday because I was going on holiday! Silly me.

Anyway we arrived at London at 9 o'clock. We went to Waterloo and to Eurostar station. We met all other people who were going on this trip. They looked kind.

I had to travel on the train for hours then at last we arrived at Lille in France. Then in the coach we travelled for about 3 hours. When we arrived there(Paris), we visited Montmartre hill we saw Basilique du Sacre-Coeur. It had been placed somewhere very high. In front of the building there was loads of steps and it seemed as if you were on top of Paris. You could see the whole city of Paris. This white building was made in 1876 and was finished in 1919. Then we visited Tour Eiffel. As I remember it was 321m high. I had to go really far to see the whole Tour Eiffel because it was so big. It looked nice in the mornings but it looked magnificent when you saw the tour at night.

We went L'Arc de Triomphe next. Napoleon built this to celebrate the battle he had won. He made it in 1806 and finished it 30 years later in 1836.

The next day we went to Louvre Museum. I saw lots of famous statues and pictures. I saw Mona Lisa by Leonardo da Vinci and saw Venus famous of her prettiness and other things too.

At Cathe'dral Notre-Dame De Paris I wasn't really listening what the guide was explaining but I can remember some bits and these are some bits.

Notredame is a word meaning Mary. This Cathedral is one of Paris's great buildings. Kings and Queens married in Notre-Dame. To make this great, great Cathedral it took lots of hard work. They built it from 1163 and finished it in 1330. That took about 200 years. It took exactly, 167 years. That's very long time. The person who planned it would have died long before it was finished!

We went around looking there and there in Avenue des Champs-Elysees. I quite liked that street at night.

The next day we set off to Geneve in Switzerland. First we went to Lac Le'man & Jet d'Eau, the lake. It's length is 72 km. It is the greatest lake in Switzerland. In May ~ September the water's length was 145m! Amazing! It's amazing.

Then we walked to Jardin Anglais, English garden which was very near. It was a very pretty park with lots of trees and flowers just like an English park. That's why they call the park English park although it's in Switzerland. In that park, there was a flower clock, which was famous. It was a real clock decorated with flowers. It was really good.

Then when we had a good look round and took photos, we moved to a Chinese restaurant for lunch. The restaurant was near Alps and after lunch we had a ride in cable car to get a nice view. It was a bit scary when we were coming down, I mean when we were going up, I thought it was great when we were going down. After the cable car journey, we headed for Italy for our next day and also our hotel was there.

Early Monday morning, we set off heading towards Pisa.

In Pisa, we visited, Duomo, the Cathedral and of course Torre Pendente (tour of Pisa), Torre Pendente is 54.5m long. Pisa is not straight it is slightly on right. So, they stopped building it but managed to finish it. It's got 294 stairs and when you go to the top of Pisa, you can get a brilliant view.

Tommy's Lost Ball

Tommy was sleeping. His mother woke him up.

His mother Mrs. Carter said to Tommy,

"Wake up, Tommy. We are going to the beach. Dress up quickly."

Tommy asked, "Mum, Can I take my new ball with me?"

Mrs. Cater replied, "Of course, Ah! your sister Luins called her friend Sally to go with us. So, you can call a friend of yours."

Tommy replied dressing up.

"Oh yes, I will call David but Oh, no, Sally's coming. I don't like Sally."

His mum said, "Come down and call David."

So, Tommy went down and rang his friend David. "Hi, Dave, I'm Tom. Are you allowed to go to the beach with my family?"

David replied, "Hello, Tommy. I am allowed. My mum said I can play with friend for an hour, that's same."

Tommy said, "Sally's coming also, By the way, come

quickly. Sally's already in our house, Bye."

Soon David came so, Tommy's family, Sally and David went.

Later they arrived.

They changed their cloth and went out. The girls were swimming at the beach and boys were playing with ball at the beach.

David threw the ball. Tommy couldn't catch it and Oh dear the ball passed too far away. David and Tommy searched everywhere at the sea. But they couldn't find it.

Tommy said to Dave, "Oh, no. I bought that yesterday. It's new one. I really liked it. It bounces like a kangaroo. Oh dear."

David said, "I'm sorry, if it was my fault Tommy."

Tommy said, "Of course not Dave. We will be able to find it later."

They searched.

Suddenly David said, "How about asking Sally and Luins for help? Tommy."

Tommy agreed.

But What a Surprise!

Sally and Luins were playing with Tommy's ball. Tommy shouted, "Oey, you bad girls Sally and Luins, Who said play with MY BALL? Luins?"

Luins laughed and said, "Tommy, Don't shout at me, Sally said."

Tommy still looked angry.

He said, "Sally said what?"

Sally replied, "I said to Luins to play with your ball. I think you have to say 'Thank you' to me?"

David said "Thank you" but Tommy didn't.

"Why are you saying 'Thank you' to them. They are naughty girls, stealing my ball."

But David smiled and said, "They found it, if it wasn't Sally, you've lost your ball! So, I said 'Thank you' to Sally and Luins."

Tommy's face went red, he said quietly to girls,

"Er... Thanks."

And I think Tommy's ball made Tommy kind and friendly to everyone.

What a good ball it was!

Present, Teacher, Su-Hyean

There was a girl called Su-Hyean, but everyone except her family called her Sue because it was easier to call her.

One day Sue's teacher said, "Right, everyone, Please put the book in your desk and look at me."

Everyone did. Mrs. Howard continued, "Tomorrow we are making something. We will need some clothes and papers. I am preparing papers You will have to prepare some cloth. Not new ones, old one. Which you don't use them, not T-shirts and Jeans, because that will be useful to you. You can give it to smaller children. So I want you to bring some old sock. See you tomorrow children."

All the children was excited but not Su-Hyean.

She had a lot of old socks but she thought everyone would laugh at her old socks.

So on her way home, she bought some new socks, and then she went home happily.

Next morning Mrs. Howard said, "Please calm down children. With a pen please put your name on your sock."

Su-Hyean putted her name with pencil because everyone had old sock except her. She didn't put the sock in the box. She thought she would put it when it's home time. At home time when everyone went home and Mrs. Howard was in Mrs. Macnaughton's class, Su-Hyean putted her socks. She ran off to her home.

At evening Su-Hyean begged to her mum.

"Mum, please can you buy me some colour pens, please mum~ Please can you buy me some colour pens."

Her mother said, "Please, Be quiet. Dad is calling with somebody. Maybe, somebody heard what you had said. Be quiet."

Next morning, Su-Hyean went to school earlier.

Mrs. Howard said to her, "Thank you for your new socks, Su-Hyean. I said to children give old socks, but I wanted to see who is kind and will bring new socks. It's you, it's for you."

Su-Hyean smiled and said thank you. Su-Hyean though it was the nicest present, that she had ever had!

The Happy Birthday

Sue was 7. She was 8 tomorrow.

Her mum Mrs. Henry said, "Sue, Give this sandwich and drink to Aunt Jim, all right? You could help Aunt Jim if you want."

Sue said holding a bag, "Auntie Jimmy who works in a Shoe Shop?"

"That's right Sue. How about inviting her in the Party tomorrow?" said Mrs. Henry.

Sue replied putting sandwich and a drink in to her small bag. "That's a good idea. I got a card for Auntie Jimmy here. Bye Mummy. I could be late but it not will be that long staying in Auntie Jimmy's Shop."

Her mum waved too. She walked down a quiet road. On her way she visited Rachel.

Sue said, "Hiya, Rachel, a card for you I might come on my way back to here to play, but I can't right now. I got to give this lunch to Auntie Jimmy. Bye bye Rachel."

Rachel said smiling when she finished reading the card.

"Thanks for inviting me, Sue, Bye. I'll have to prepare nice cloth for tomorrow and brilliant present for you."

Rachel waved, Sue waved as well. She went right and saw Aunt Jim's Shoes Shop and went in.

Sue said, "Hello, Auntie Jimmy, here's something from me also."

Aunt Jim said proudly eating, "Oh, you're so kind to invite me and thank you very much for my lunch dear Sue. Sue, look at this. It's new fashioned trainer, I made it today. What do you think about it, dear Sue?"

Sue replied, "That's a wonderful fashion, Auntie Jimmy but I don't like it's colour. I don't like red. It will be nicer if it is very bright blue."

Aunt Jim said sighing, "I don't like hearing you don't like this. I will choose shoes for you, nice shoes. You will like shoes for birthday present, don't you?"

Sue said sitting in a chair, "Of course Auntie Jimmy. I don't like my old little trainer."

Auntie Jim smiled. Then a visitor came, so Sue went home.

Next day, the party was in Legoland, all children played and when it was dark they went to Sue's house and had a tea. Everyone gave Sue a present. Rachel gave a big crystal ball,

Callum gave her a teddy bear, Luke gave her a hair band, Amy gave Sue a book called 'There was a girl called SUE'. It looked very exciting. Charotte gave her a badge which says 'Happy Birthday to you'. Jack gave her a note book and Auntie Jim gave her marvellous shoes it was very new fashion and was bright blue. The light came out when she walked.

She thought it was so Amazing Party she ever had.

Blame Everywhere

chapter 1

Dan sat on a bench near the pond in the Edge Hill Park. He did not want to go to his house. He knew the blame would start.

Sometimes he spent his times with Mickey his best friend but today he couldn't. Mickey moved away not so far away and he moved his school also.

Dan now had no one to play with in the school. Mickey was Dan's best person. He knew the feeling that Dan had when Dan got blamed because Mickey had blamed also. He slowly walked to his house. He soon arrived. He pressed the bell, his mother shouted. "Who are you?"

Dan said nothing.

"Who are you?" asked his mum again.

"I'm Dan mum. I'm back."

His big sister Luis opened the door. Dan went in. Aha! The twins ran to him. Eric and Linny.

He liked them. They were one of his favourite person.

"Daniel," cried Eric.

"Welcome, Welcome." cried Linny.

Dan went upstairs to his bedroom, he sat on a chair. Dan started doing his homework. His concentration let him forgot about the blame.

chapter 2

"Aaaaryh"

Dan heard a scream. It was his mum's.

He have to go down whenever he heard a scream.

It was family rule. Everyone came down including Eric and Linny also.

"What's the matter mum?" asked Luis.

"Look at my best dish! Oh."

"Gosh! Daniel! Punishment is waiting for you! Tidy my bedroom." shouted Luis.

"Play with me." It was Eric's punishment. Nice punishment.

"Mend my teddy Daniel." said Linny.

"A piece is missing! Dear, it mean I never will stick it together!" yelled Dan's mum.

Dan was really sad. He done nothing. He never went to the kitchen at this afternoon.

What a terrible blame!

And what a horrible punishment that Luis gave to Dan!!

Dan first went to Linny's bedroom.

He found the teddy which had an eye off. He got some glue and stuck the eye. Easy-Peasy.

Dan, then went to Eric's room.

Eric said, "Danny, Punishment."

"That's why I came to your room," replied Dan.

"Yes!" said Eric. "Make me two paper aeroplane."

Dan got some paper from his room. He was used to make lots of aeroplane when he was age of Eric.

He made it and gave it to Eric. Eric looked happy. Easy-Peasy.

It was time to do horriblest punishment.

Dan knocked Luis's bedroom door.

"Come!"

Dan went in. Luis shouted.

"Right, naughty boy, tidy my room."

Was Luis room a dust bin?

How messy it was!

Luis went out and Dan started clean the Luis's room. When he was about to go out, he saw a glass!

A piece of plate!

Dan's mum's piece of plate!

Dan put the piece in his pocket.

He went down to his mum.

"Finished... Finished? Daniel!" called Luis.

"Yes, Luis. Don't shout at me liar," said Dan.

"Naughty boy. Shut up." and Luis went to her bedroom.

"Mum?..." said Dan quite confidently.

"What? Naughty boy?" said Dan's mum without looking at Dan.

"Look..." He took out the piece.

Dan's mum looked. She didn't say anything.

"I found it from Luis's room when I was tiding her room."

"Can I trust you?..." asked Dan's mum.

Dan nodded.

"Luis! Naughty girl!" Shouted Dan's mum.

Luis got terrible punishment and after this no one ever blamed Dan.

A Lucky Day

James Pruy lived near a beach. One day his little brother Tommy came in and took James's favourite hat while James was sleeping when it was already 10 o'clock. Tommy took the hat to the garden and played with it. When Tommy went into the house, he forgot to take the hat with him.

When James wake up, he was thinking to go to Jordon's house to show his new hat. He searched for the hat but couldn't find it. So he asked to Tommy.

"Tom. Tom!" shouted James desperately.

"What? What?" replied Tommy.

"Have you seen my new hat?" said James.

"Er...Yes." Tommy thought about it. He had played with it and left it.

Tommy decided to tell the truth.

"Well, I played with your hat and I left it in the garden."

"You idiot! Without my permission!"

James was very angry. He went out. He thought there

wasn't the hat because it had flew away with the wind. He didn't want to go to Jordon's. He wanted to go to Arthur's house.

DING DONG , DING DONG

Arthur opened the door.

"Hi! do you want to go to the beach with me?" asked Arthur cheerfully.

"Sure," replied James feebly remembering his hat again.

They went to the beach. What a Surprise!

How shocking.

There was James' hat waiting for him!

THE END

THE WONDERFUL STORY CLUB

초판 1쇄 발행 2018년 2월 12일

지은이 ShinJi Park
펴낸이 강수걸
기획 이수현
편집장 권경옥
편집 정선재 윤은미 박하늘바다 김향남 이송이
디자인 권문경 조은비
펴낸곳 산지니
등록 2005년 2월 7일 제333-3370000251002005000001호
주소 부산시 해운대구 수영강변대로 140 BCC 613호
전화 051-504-7070 | 팩스 051-507-7543
홈페이지 www.sanzinibook.com
전자우편 sanzini@sanzinibook.com
블로그 http://sanzinibook.tistory.com

ISBN 978-89-6545-485-4 03810

* 책값은 뒤표지에 있습니다.